REESE GABRIEL

Temporary Slave

Ellora's Cave
Romantica Publishing

TEMPORARY SLAVE
An Ellora's Cave Publication, April 2005

Ellora's Cave Publishing, Inc.
1337 Commerce Drive, Suite #13
Stow, Ohio 44224

ISBN #1419951106

Other available formats: ISBN MS Reader (LIT), Adobe (PDF), Rocketbook (RB), Mobipocket (PRC) & HTML

Edited by: *Pamela Campbell*
Cover art by: *Syneca*

What the critics are saying...

"*Temporary Slave* is a fantastic novel!! I just loved it!!... The love scenes were extremely powerful...erotic, passionate, and so explosive it was just HOT! Keep a glass of water nearby because *Temporary Slave* is a story that will ignite your passion and maybe your curiosity into the life of BDSM." ~ *Susan Holly Just Erotic Romance Reviews*

"*Temporary Slave* simply leaves a blazing trail on your fingers...You'll be sweating and squirming in your chair in no time...This is one unforgettable and scorching read." ~ *Aggie Tsirikas Just Erotic Romance Reviews*

Warning:

The following material contains graphic sexual content meant for mature readers. *Temporary Slave* has been rated *E-rotic* by a minimum of three independent reviewers.

Ellora's Cave Publishing offers three levels of Romantica™ reading entertainment: S (S-ensuous), E (E-rotic), and X (X-treme).

S-e*nsuous* love scenes are explicit and leave nothing to the imagination.

E-*rotic* love scenes are explicit, leave nothing to the imagination, and are high in volume per the overall word count. In addition, some E-rated titles might contain fantasy material that some readers find objectionable, such as bondage, submission, same sex encounters, forced seductions, etc. E-rated titles are the most graphic titles we carry; it is common, for instance, for an author to use words such as "fucking", "cock", "pussy", etc., within their work of literature.

X-*treme* titles differ from E-rated titles only in plot premise and storyline execution. Unlike E-rated titles, stories designated with the letter X tend to contain controversial subject matter not for the faint of heart.

Also by Reese Gabriel:

Dance of Submission

Kimerlee's Keeper

Roping His Filly

Come and Get Me

Temporary Slave

Chapter One

I will not imagine the new CEO using me as his sex slave. I will not imagine the new CEO using me as his sex slave…

The mantra was too little, too late. Red-haired, long-legged Meridian Hunter, her heart thumping like a rabbit's, was losing herself to her libido. Her conscious mind had checked out of the staff meeting, the figure of her blue-eyed boss standing at the head of the conference table in his smart gray suit replacing itself with quite a different vision of the man. He was a pirate captain now.

His short, lustrously dark hair was as wavy as the sea. His eyes were as deep as the sky, and he had tanned skin that smelled vaguely of salt and rum. His white shirt was open nearly to the waist, revealing a finely muscled chest. He wore a sword and pearl-handled dagger at his side, attached with a thick belt, black and glossy like his high boots.

She was his prisoner, a fair maiden captured at sea. They were below deck on his dreaded pirate's galleon, in his cabin, a place of rough wood and strong male essence. So far he had not touched her person, nor even tied her with rope, but there was no mistaking her place in his world—helpless, dependent upon him for her very breath.

"I am at your mercy," she confessed, feeling strangely uncovered in her tight-waisted gown of green velvet. "Though surely you know my father will pay handsomely for my return?"

The brigand smiled thinly, clearly amused as he regarded his disarrayed prisoner, her ruined red tresses hanging about her shoulders, the bodice of her expensive dress torn, revealing just the tiniest bit of her milk-white bosom. "I've enough gold in my coffers, already. My needs are of a different nature, my dear."

Panic welled in her breast as she regarded the strange, predatory glint in his eyes, not to mention the swell in his tight breeches. It was well known what pirates were capable of doing to captured damsels lost at sea. Still, she hoped to appeal to the gentleman in him.

"Sir, I am a virgin, and beg you, lay not your hands upon me, though I be powerless to keep you from raping me."

"Rape?" He tipped back his head, the laughter deep and rich. "Do you think I would go through such trouble as to sink your ship to apprehend you just for a few minutes of stolen pleasure? Oh, no, my angel, it is all of you I desire, body and soul."

Meridian turned a shade paler than her natural porcelain. "I do not catch your meaning, sir."

"I have captured you to be my slave," he explained. "Is that not obvious?"

She shook her head, trying to hide her desperation. "I think you must have mistaken me for some common wench. I am the daughter of the Earl of—"

"Silence!" he commanded.

She watched him take a short leather whip from the foot of his bed. She had not noticed it before. "What do you intend to do with that, sir?"

"I shall redden your behind with it," he slashed the device through the air. "If you do not at once remove your clothing and fall before me in submission."

Meridian fought the overwhelming tide of arousal at the thought of being nude, and in this man's sexual clutches. "I would sooner die," she vowed.

The pirate moved the whip to his left hand and drew his blade with the right. "That can be arranged."

She fell to her knees, begging—the age-old ploy of the defeated female. "Please, sir, my father is very rich. He will give you whatever you want."

"He already has," the pirate grinned. "He has given me you. From this moment forward, you will consider yourself my private property. You will remain in my cabin, at my beck and call. You will serve my sexual whims and otherwise keep my quarters spotlessly clean. Disobedience or failure to satisfy in any way will result in punishment, either from me or my crew."

She held up her hands in an attitude of prayer. "My Lord Captain, if you have any sense of honor, spare me."

The handsome pirate lifted her chin with the tip of his blade, applying sufficient pressure to bring her quickly back to her feet. "What I have is a long, hard cock and a short temper. Now strip."

Meridian continued her useless bargaining even as she undid the fastenings of her dress. "If you wish," she offered, "we could arrange for my hand in marriage. Then I would be legally yours."

"Legally?" he scoffed. "And what use has a pirate for the law? That's for landlubbers, and rich ones at that."

The scoundrel made her take off everything, even her pantaloons. When she was stark naked, he sheathed his sword.

"Do you have any experience pleasing a man's cock?" She turned as red as a beet, insisting a well-bred young lady like her would never stoop to such an action.

"That's too bad," he informed her. "Some skill in that area would have served you well. As it is, you are liable to take a striping or two 'til you get it right."

She gasped in awe as he pulled out his member, thick and fat, pulsing with veins and tapering to a delicious, uncircumcised head. Never had she seen a man in this state and she could scarcely imagine how this part of him could be in any way accommodated by her small, female body.

"Mercy," she whispered, though deep inside her, she was feeling a beckoning heat, as if a part of her wanted this. To be used. And owned. And disgraced.

"Slaves are not entitled to mercy." He snapped the whip across her hip, just hard enough to make her yelp. "To the bed," he ordered. "It's time to earn your keep."

This sudden, cruel blow, apparently, was the man's idea of a gentle hint to prepare for the taking of her virginity. She had no doubt that were she to disobey, he would use whatever further persuasion he needed to accomplish the job. This thought alone was enough to open her and soften her in a way that made her blush to her core.

"Let's try a sample of that tight virgin pussy," he said amiably. "Then we'll see about that pretty mouth of yours. You will call me 'Master' from now on."

Meridian lay upon the pirate's bed. He ordered her to spread her legs, baring her pink sex. She watched, mesmerized, as he stroked himself in preparation to take his pleasure. "It will hurt a little at first," he explained, "but you will come to enjoy it. In time, you will learn to beg, even."

The man's cock was so long and hard, designed so perfectly for her domination. Her tiny naked body trembled before its majesty. It was here that her slavery would become real, for she knew she would have to please him well or face his wrath.

"I'd advise you to relax," he said, climbing astride her. "You'll only make it harder on yourself if you fight me."

He went straight for her breast, sucking it hard. She moaned as his teeth clenched on her nipple.

"Oh, god," she thrashed miserably. "What are you doing to me?"

"Hold still," he complained, grabbing her wrists. Leather straps were attached to the headboard. In a matter of moments he had her arms secured over her head and wide apart.

She pulled at her restraints in disbelief. Only a whore would be treated in such a way. "Sir, please, do not shame me this way."

His hand moved between her legs, finding her wet and ready. "You are a slave," he informed her. "You will accustom yourself to being taken in bondage."

Meridian groaned as he took hold of her clitoris, delivering spasms of sweet pain.

"You have neglected to call me Master," he reminded.

"Forgive me," she cried. "Master."

The pirate's finger worked her to a furious lather, reducing her to whimpers in a few seconds. "I will not go easy on you," he warned. "Virgin or not. You will take my cock to the hilt and in a single thrust. Is that clear?"

"Yes, Master."

The pirate poised himself at the opening to her pussy. His gaze was dark and filled with lust. Closing her eyes, Meridian concentrated on submitting, on thinking of what he was going to do to her now, and later, and how that made her feel like melting snow at the touch of summer heat.

"I claim you now, wench," he said decisively, thrusting himself inside her. "You are mine from this moment forward."

"Oh, god," she moaned, the sounds caught in her throat as he buried himself in her warm hole. At the exact same moment, he grabbed her breasts, squeezing them hard. The combination of the sensations set her to undulating and spasming. Unable to help herself, she began to plead with the man to allow her to come.

"Earn it," he told her. "Earn it, my slave."

"Yessss, Master." She took him deeper, melting…so good, so strong and so…

"Miss Hunter, are you with us?"

Meridian nearly leaped from her seat at the sound of Marshall Wilder's voice, rich, raspy and bordering on irritation. He was every bit the modern pirate. Imperious, perfectly formed, weathered by hostile takeovers and leveraged buyouts. The tailored silk business suit was a substitute for the long coat and breeches, while the strong lips, the jaw, the wide shoulders and tapered waist, not to mention the eagle eyes and capable, commanding hands, all were straight out of her fantasy.

She could still picture him, still naked, looming over her, lean and ready, the consummate warrior, prepared to make his mark. Only now, it wasn't her sex he was pinning down, it was her mind.

Her pale features pinkened from the sudden flash of embarrassment. The man had caught her sexually fantasizing in the middle of a staff meeting. And about him, no less. Swallowing hard she looked up into his eyes.

Cerulean blue, hard and piercing. Like a Mediterranean sky or the rolling tide of the endless sea. Mysterious, depthless and infinitely alive. The perfect compliment to the jet-black hair and ruddy features. Oh god, Meridian was so lost right now.

There was no wiggle room. No pretense of equality or androgyny. He would take what he wanted, use what he wanted. He was every bit the male in the situation and he made no bones about the differences between them.

This left only one role for her. The female. Soft and small...and hunted.

The pink on her cheeks turned to crimson. Was he seeing into her thoughts? Could he read her mind enough to know she was imagining such things...wicked, nasty things—with him playing the part of sadistic tormentor and her, the hapless victim, used and conquered, readied for a life of sexual servitude and slavish obedience?

"Absolutely, sir, I'm with you all the way," she barely avoided calling him Master. "The Philmont account. Don't worry, the creative team is right on top of that one."

The new owner of Dream Image Advertising and Consulting arched a single, rakish black brow, sharp as a rapier. The motion in turn caused the lines of his handsome face to tighten very slightly, multiplying the effect, challenging and ominous.

Part of her wanted to run, but another part felt drawn to him, like a moth to flame—drawn to the storms raging behind those eyes. Was she reading too much into the expression, or could she see the etchings of pain, hurt he kept to himself? The rest of the staff lived in dread, but there were times—moments at least—when she thought she saw something warm at the edges of the sharp angles, kinks in the armor, or signs, perhaps, of thawing glaciers to come. If so, that would make for quite a flood.

"Philmont was five minutes ago, Miss Hunter. We've moved on to the Morrissey Brewing account. If it's not too much trouble for you."

Merrie tried unsuccessfully to melt into the leather boardroom chair. "No trouble, sir," she said meekly, feeling like a little girl who'd just been chastised by daddy.

It wasn't the first time she'd felt this way with the charismatic Wilder, not by a long shot. Never before had a boss—a man—made her so uncomfortable and rendered her so darned incompetent. It made no sense. She was a VP for heaven's sake, with five years experience in the company. She'd worked her way up, earned everything she had the hard way, tempering ambition with professionalism and respect. She had goals, long-range plans. And here he'd come in out of nowhere, owning the business for all of two weeks.

What was she so worried about? He was only one person, a human being who put his pants on one leg at a time.

Okay, so maybe he was impossibly cool and chiseled, square-jawed and totally physically fit, so much so that her libido blew a gasket when he took his shirt off at the company basketball game.

All that bronzed skin, lean, Adonis-like, the drops of sweat beading on those smooth pectorals, dripping enticingly down a yummy, washboard belly to the waistband of tight elastic shorts. And what a competitor. It was as if his life hung on every point. It was at these moments, in the fierceness of battle, that he looked the sexiest. Like a sleek and sinewy tiger, studying its prey, moving with smart and deadly efficiency, waiting for the opportune moment to strike. Her mouth would water with every jump he made, every twist of his sweaty torso and with each movement of his muscular thighs as he mastered the court, end to end.

But, she noticed something else, too. He was always an excellent sport and he tolerated no complaints on his side about the rulings. Fouls by teammates against his opponents were dealt with sternly as well. He brooked no mistreatment of the rival team. Without fail, he showed everyone the utmost respect and it didn't matter if you were a VP or a custodian, out there on the court, you were an equal.

Merry knew this meant the man had some sort of ethics, though they seemed to be reserved for other males and they followed rules she did not understand. He played to win, but he did not cheat. Just seeing all this, watching him in this world of testosterone would make her so horny she would invariably spend the nights after the games masturbating.

She would picture him taking her, covered in sweat, grabbing her and looking her in the eye, overcoming her with his desires before pushing her down onto the floor to serve him. Oh, how she would wonder who really was enjoying the fruit of all that lust.

He had no love interest that anyone knew of and he showed no particular sexual interest in any of his employees, her included.

Rumor was he'd been through a bitter divorce and had sworn off the opposite sex entirely. In Merrie's mind, and that of every other red-blooded female in the company, it was a waste bordering on the criminal.

But Merrie had an extra special problem of her own, because unbeknownst to anyone, the man bore a striking resemblance to a tall, dark and domineering figure out of her teenage fantasies.

It had been years since she'd thought of being bound, commanded and treated as little more than a sex toy by a powerful, masterful man. Work had cured her of that illusion, and before that a lot of college drinking and really piss-poor relationships with a series of spineless worms and mama's boys.

One by one, she'd tested her men and they'd failed. A little teasing on her part and they'd been reduced to begging, a few mind games and they would whine for mercy. Just once she wanted a man strong enough to kiss her silly, to not expect her to make all the decisions in bed. A man who knew what he wanted and could get it from a woman—leaving her screaming for more in the process.

In time she learned this was a real-life impossibility. The combination she sought was something found only in fairy tales. Strong-willed men were bullies and sensitive ones had no backbone. So she made herself a nun of sorts. Burying her sexual needs deep inside.

Only now it was all rushing back to the surface—in the person of Marshall Wilder. She simply could not help herself. The man had charisma, a raw confidence and power. One story had him staring down a local mafia boss after he'd demanded protection money not to disrupt Marshall's first business, a construction company. A much younger Wilder had taken a few of his toughest men and gone to pay the don a visit. By the time they were through, the mob boss had been convinced to leave him and the rest of the neighborhood alone.

And yet this same Marshall Wilder was capable of treating her and the other employees like his personal slaves. In his eyes, she already felt like a possession. The question was, what kind exactly?

He was a walking contradiction, that's what he was. At times seeming indifferent and faraway, consumed by invisible troubles, at others focused on some minute detail with a ferocity that defied understanding. Almost brutally coarse at one moment and the next showing surprising mercy.

To cut costs, for example, he'd sacked half the art staff, and then he'd turned around and given one of them, a father with a newborn baby a severance package of nearly a hundred thousand dollars just for coming to him and pleading his case.

"We're going to nail Morrissey," she announced, trying not to fixate on his crotch. "The pitch should be ready by tomorrow noon."

In her fantasies, Meridian would serve that cock of his. As her Master, Wilder would snap his fingers and she would go to her knees. Eyes gazing up at his, full of love and devotion, she would part her lips in eager anticipation of worshipping his thick, veined cock, her soft mouth sliding up and down the sculpted hardness, the bulbous head slipping inside, sweetly and commandingly.

"Make it by ten," Wilder said curtly, the motion of his full lips, tight and decisive sending a shiver down Merrie's spine. What would lips like that do to her poor body? Her earlobes? Her breasts? Her nipples?

Marshall turned his attention elsewhere. "Johnson, where in blazes are those monthly revenue figures?"

Avery Johnson pushed his wire-rim glasses up his small nose nervously. "Sir, the month doesn't close 'til today."

Marshall scowled, looking like Meridian's pirate about to sink a schooner. "Estimate it, man, estimate it. I want the figures on my desk in an hour. You can stay tonight and work it up for real."

Johnson's shoulders slumped. "Yes, sir."

What a bastard, thought Merrie. Doesn't he know the man has kids? Little League? Ballet practice? Just because he has no life and works twenty hours a day doesn't mean everyone has to.

"Is there a problem, Miss Hunter?"

Every eye in the boardroom was on her. Most especially his. Imperiously blue, tight as laser beams, twice as nasty. *Oh god,* she thought, *he must be reading my mind again.* Was there no escaping his purview? Was he going to keep at her until she had no choice but to blurt out her need to be stripped and ravished by him? Did he really want to reduce her to a panting, needy…female?

"Well… I was just thinking how Avery has the soccer carpool for his little boy and—"

"Good. You'll do the report for him." Wilder pressed the intercom button calling for his personal assistant. "Sharon, more coffee."

Merrie sat there stunned, waiting for the punch line. "But Mr. Wilder, I'm not an accountant."

"Bloody well learn," he thundered. "Meeting's over. Stop wasting my money," he pointed to the door. "And get back to work, all of you."

The executive staff scurried out like so many church mice.

"Not you, Hunter."

Merrie froze in the doorway.

I will not imagine the new CEO spanking my bare buttocks…I will not imagine myself over his knee being punished; I will not, I will not. I will not…

"Sit," he pointed to the leather couch like she was a pet spaniel.

Merrie did so gingerly, trying to tug her skirt down as far as possible over her long dancer's legs, still toned from too many years of tap and jazz as a kid.

Wilder's eyes strayed to them for a second, inducing another frown on his part. Did he not approve of her attire? Wild thoughts passed through her mind of the man punishing her for revealing too much skin. Ordering her to bend over his desk and lift up her skirt.

"Take down your panties, Miss Hunter," he'd command, in the same superior tone he used on Sharon and everyone else. Her skin would tingle in response. Her thighs would flood with moisture.

"What are you going to do to me?" She would whisper, even as she slid down the tiny cotton garment, exposing herself.

"I'm going to teach you a lesson, young woman. Brace yourself."

"Oh, sir," she would moan. "I'm scared..."

And then it would happen. Her world changed with a single crack of his hand on her wriggling behind. Her whimpers and pleas ignored, he would do as he wished, punishing, correcting...and arousing.

The real Wilder cleared his throat pointedly.

"Whatever's going on between us, Miss Hunter," he yanked loose the Windsor knot of his silk print tie, and took off his jacket. "It stops here. Got it?"

Merrie squeezed her thighs together. He looked just like the pirate now, stripped to his shirt, standing, looming, the sinews of his neck exposed, giving just enough of a hint of his bare chest to leave her craving more. Merrie's nipples were hard bullets under her white blouse. Did this man have any idea of the effect he had on her? It was all she could do to keep from sliding off the sofa to the floor at his feet, begging for his touch, all over her body, anywhere he wanted, taking, teasing.

"I'm not aware of any issues, sir..."

Nothing that couldn't be settled by you ripping my clothes off and having me on this sofa, she thought sardonically. The Wilder brow, famous for intimidating plutocrats and princes on three continents, furrowed to offensive mode.

"Like hell, you aren't. I'll give you ten minutes and you had better have an answer for me. Or else your resignation."

Merrie just sat there watching, feeling like she was in a movie about her own life. The man had turned away from her. He was calm as could be, rolling up his sleeves. Finally he sat down in his leather chair to read correspondence at his desk. *Great, she thought, I'm eleven again, sitting in the principal's office.*

Except she was not a child and this was no principal. A potentate with the body of a male model, an exasperating tyrannical CEO, yes, but not a pedagogue.

Wilder scribbled notes here and there with an ink pen, the seconds ticking by. Merrie did not want to lose her job. She had to give him something, anything. The trouble was, all she could focus on were his forearms, lightly haired and smoothly muscled. In her opinion, they needed to be kissed, as did the rest of him.

Sharon came in, blonde, busty and old enough to know better.

"Sir, your coffee," she bowed, giving him an eyeful down the V-neck of her low-cut sweater. "Is there anything else I can do for you?"

Merrie had serious problems with Sharon, not only for being just the kind of female every man wanted, but for encouraging the man to treat her like his personal servant. She fetched him food, picked up his laundry, and Merrie was quite sure she would do other things, too, offering up her body for his entertainment if he wanted it.

She liked that Marshall seemed oblivious to her. Maybe that was catty on Merrie's part. There might have been a twinge of jealousy at the access Sharon had to him. Truth be told, she had a particular fantasy of her own about being the man's "personal" assistant, emphasis on the personal.

"Time's up," Marshall said finally, his tone only a tiny bit more civil than that of the pirate captain in her fantasy.

"The previous owners were talking about turning over day-to-day operations," she blurted, the situation having pushed her past her normal limits of caution.

He peered at her over the top of his reading spectacles, which he'd donned to check the mail. They seemed strangely out of place on a man who looked as young as he did. Then again, she had to remember he was forty-five to her thirty-six. "And?"

Here goes nothing, she thought. "And...they were going to turn things over...to me."

Merrie braced herself. Zero to fired in less than sixty seconds.

"All right. Fine."

She blinked. "Fine?"

"Write a proposal, Miss Hunter. No promises. And don't look like a deer in front of headlights. You think I'm going to stay here forever? This company is barely a blip on my radar. Once I get it on its feet, I'm moving on. That's how I do things."

Merrie braced herself, waiting for the other shoe to drop.

Marshall sighed, sensing her suspicion. "Look, Miss Hunter," he continued, his tone a bit more subdued. "I'm not sure what you've been told about me and frankly I don't care. I'm not here to be liked and if you ever sit in this chair, I don't want you to care, either. When I was eighteen, I got my start in business. Three days I waited outside the front door of a certain man's office building. He was the best and I was determined to work for him. Finally, he noticed me. I had to run alongside his car to talk to him. I told him I'd take any job he had. He scribbled a name on a piece of paper, told me to report in the morning. I went to work digging ditches for one of his crews. Sixty hours a week, rain or shine. Six months later, he checked to see if I was still there. I was, so he gave me a job as an assistant to his executive assistant. Three years later, I was running a whole division for him. Two more years and I'd bought him out. That's what it's all about. Not being polite or mealymouthed. You catch my drift?"

Merry tried very hard not to picture the man digging those ditches, his bronzed torso swinging those tools all day in the hot sun, herself, waiting naked on her knees to bring him water, to lick the sweat from his body and suck dry his cock whenever he needed it.

"Yes, sir, I do."

He examined her a moment, as if he were going to say something more, then decided against it." Goodbye, Miss Hunter," he dismissed, the lowered eyebrows leaving no question as to the finality of the meeting. "I want the report on my desk. Eight a.m. sharp."

Merrie stopped in the hall for a much-needed drink of water from the fountain. She was not sure what had overwhelmed her most, what Marshall had said or the way he'd looked when saying it. Just being in a room alone with the man was enough to make a woman swoon. How did Sharon do it all day long? The way he focused, his eyes so clear, his jaw never wavering, like they were in the final three seconds of one of his basketball games and he was about to pass her the ball.

A man like this held nothing back, and right or wrong he wouldn't fail for lack of trying. If that wasn't integrity, she didn't know what was. And yet he left no room for listening, just dictating. No one else could be fast enough, on top of things enough. It made her want to stand up and shout at the top of her lungs. It made her want to write up a ten-page list of all his faults.

It made her want to be with him, too, in the worst way, tearing off his clothes—and hers—to get at him, putting all of this stuff between them into the one arena they had yet to try. The one arena where rank did not matter.

Or did it?

Merrie made it back to her office zombie-like. Shooing off her well-meaning intern, Kennedy Fontaine, she closed the door behind her. Talk about being a bundle of contradicting emotions. On the one hand, this was the moment Meridian had been waiting two years for. She had it all mapped out in her head. Down to the last detail of how she could save the company tens of thousands of dollars, increase business and streamline operations by nearly twenty percent, all within the first year.

Except she'd planned to make her pitch to Sam and Lyla Hughes, the old owners, not this twenty-first century pirate who made her knees weak every time he walked into the room. How would she present anything to this kind of man? In Marshall Wilder's presence, she didn't feel like any kind of executive, but merely a woman, being calmly appraised in his eyes. It was unnerving. Degrading…and incredibly hot.

Yet she had not one scrap of evidence that the man had any sexual interest in her, or that he even regarded her as anything more than a mild insect-like annoyance.

What about that ditch digging story, though? Was that supposed to mean something? Was it some veiled way to encourage her, or just another weapon in his

arsenal of intimidation? She'd be damned if she cou
the man. His emotions were locked up tighter tha
Knox. In a way, he was the perfect billboard figur
magazine model. The quintessential masculine image,
cowboy or astronaut, undaunted, never cruel, smal
minded, or petty in spirit, but level, steady, approachable.

Assuming, of course, that you did so on his terms. He was the man all men wanted to be, and the man all women wanted to be with.

Something was being triggered in her, that was for sure. Today's little episode wasn't the first time Marshall Wilder had put her through paces in her imagination. And they weren't just the old tying and kidnap fantasies of her college years, either. These were extreme fantasies of being under the man's complete control.

What would it be like? she wondered. Wilder was known as being utterly ruthless in business; what would such a man demand of his bedmates? And what woman could ever hope to refuse his commands, no matter how graphic or degrading they might be? Closing her eyes, her body safely tucked into her desk chair, she tried to imagine himself responding to those eyes, that demanding voice, arrogant and totally domineering. Leaning back against the plush material, she let nature take its course.

Trance-like, Meridian touched her nipples through the blouse. They responded at once, coming to life. It was as if he was there, doing this himself. Marking her. Making her his. Deep inside, a new fantasy began to take shape, her memories reworked by raw desire.

They are in the conference room, and Wilder has just caught her not paying attention.

ss Hunter, please stand, so that everyone can see liss Hunter is a discipline problem," he said to the s, all males.

"Why am I being singled out? You're angry with veryone." The very word discipline made her weak and wet, in ways she couldn't explain.

"Because you're female," he countered, in blatant violation of every standard of nondiscrimination.

"That's not fair," she pouted. Not realizing that this only set her apart from the men. She felt so vulnerable and aroused. It was scandalous, but so very delicious.

"Step back from the table, and unbutton your blouse," he growled.

"Please don't make me do this," she begged, not wanting to degrade herself.

"Obey me, or you will face far worse," he warned, his voice stern, his eyes solidly on her. She knew he was up to the challenge of controlling her. She knew, too, that he wanted her. He was hard beneath his trousers and his pupils were dilated.

Merrie took off her blouse and put it on the table.

"What do you think?" Wilder tore his gaze away, turning to the other men.

"Man, what I wouldn't give to see those breasts," said Childs from accounting.

"Yes, yes, the breasts," agreed McNamara, massaging a monstrous hard-on.

Merrie could feel their desire and lust. She wanted to be taken and used.

Turning back, he continued. "Take off your bra, and place your hands on top of your head."

Her breathing quickened. Feeling numb, she obeyed. Cool air wafted over her breasts.

"Naughty females can be punished," he purred. "On their breasts. With clamps. And clips. And yours are so pretty, not too big, not too small."

Merrie whimpered and covered herself.

"Put your hands down, and take off your skirt," he rapped out the order.

She unbuttoned the waistband, and the skirt slid to the floor. Her panties were pink and frilly and constituted, at the moment, the worst kind of humiliation.

"Women are made for sex, gentlemen," he told his staff. "They were put on the earth to give us pleasure. They must be treated accordingly, as valuable, trainable pets."

Though rankled by his demeaning description, she felt weak and indescribably stimulated. How could such a cruel man excite her so?

"Touch yourself," Marshall ordered. "Put your hand down into your panties and show us how aroused you are."

Trembling, obeying him, she slid her hand into her panties. She moaned at her own touch. Her pussy was a spasming torrent of liquid. Shamed to the core, she removed her glistening fingers.

"You see," he said. "She loves being displayed like this. She wants to be owned. And used."

"No," she objected vehemently.

"You are not permitted to speak without permission," he snapped.

Her pussy flooded. She lowered her eyes. The others saw her like this…obeying. Wilder snapped his fingers and ordered her to come to him. Unsteadily, in panties and high heels only, she walked around the large polished oak table. The eyes of the men follow her, evaluating, mentally trying her out as a sex partner. She knew she was in Wilder's hands alone—her fate, her body. Will he take her himself or maybe give her to the others, making her surrender herself over the large table?

He had her come to within just a few inches of him. She was painfully aware of his large, powerful body. Well-exercised, disciplined and beautiful in the way only a man's body can be. They were not equals, in any sense of the word. She was smaller, less muscular, and nearly naked to boot.

"How shall I punish you, Miss Hunter?"

Her tummy fluttered. Her nipples pointed at him, painfully aroused. "I-I don't know," she whispered.

"You're an intelligent woman. Surely you have some ideas."

"I could be spanked," she mumbled, looking at her feet.

He lifted her chin between his fingers. "What did you say?"

"You could…spank me," she replied, breathless.

He eyed her, fixing her in place. The place she occupied in his mind and in reality as his plaything. "Remove your panties, Miss Hunter."

She slid the bit of pink silk down over her buttocks and her pussy. Shimmying them down her hips and legs, she let them fall to her ankles.

"Give them to me," he commanded.

She handed them over, ashamed at how wet fragrant they were. He didn't crack a smile as he toss them to the nearest man. She marveled at his will. He indeed like a statue of a king or god, timeless and immortal, yet human, a leader of real, vibrant men.

"Pass them around," he ordered. "Let's all get a good whiff of Miss Hunter's true nature."

She could see that his eyes filled with lust and it drove her wild. She wanted him to take her, but she was not ready to beg.

"What if I give you to every man in this room?" he wondered aloud. "Would that be punishment, or a treat?"

"Please," she entreated earnestly, "don't do that."

"Then you'll have to surrender to me absolutely."

Merrie fell to her knees. It felt like the most natural thing in the world. Longingly she looked up at him, at his narrow waist, the swell of his cock beneath his trousers tapering up to the nicely muscled torso under the dress shirt.

He caressed the top of her head and extending his hand. "Kiss it, Meridian."

Such a strong, vibrant hand. She could tell he had done real work with it, yet still maintained his status as a gentleman. She touched her lips to his hand and showered it lovingly with kisses. Like a good employee. A good slave.

"Stand up," he ordered. "Bend over and grab your ankles."

He had to help her to her feet because she was so weak-kneed. His grip was strong, but not hard. He was gentle in his own way.

"What will you do to me?" she whispered.

He turned her about. "You already know."

Indeed, she could make a few guesses.

Down she went, putting herself into position, bent over, completely vulnerable, her hair hanging to the floor, her fingers tightly gripping her slender ankles. Immediately, his hand caressed her ass, making her shiver.

"A woman who knows she can be spanked and taken at will," he pointed out, "is a very, very horny woman."

She moaned as he pressed a finger to her clit. It was all she could do to stay upright. The sensations, the deep pleasures, were enough to tear her world apart.

"Don't move," he warned. She shivered at the sound of his zipper sliding down.

Merrie cried out as he smacked her hard with the palm of his hand. She was being disciplined. Her pussy was gaping, hot like fire. She needed it badly. He knew this, too, as he taunted her.

"Tell me what you want."

"Y-You…inside me."

"Pretty please…" he goaded her.

"Oh, god, please," she groaned. "Take me."

Another spank on her tender buttocks. "I'll do what I want, when I want," he declared.

"Yes, Master."

"I am doing this with everyone watching, so they will know you're my property."

"Y-Yes, Master."

His hands grabbed her hips. The same hands that gripped the basketball, launching it through the net, the same hands that thrummed the conference table in impatience at a sloppy job, or pointed to the graphs on the wall, showing the way to the future. And now, they'd be the hands that claimed her.

She felt his naked cock poised at her entrance. Desperately, she thrust her ass back against him. He squeezed her hips, forcing her to stay still.

"Quit squirming. Do you want to be paddled?" His voice was firm, not harsh.

"No, please, Master…mercy," she begged.

His cock slid an inch between her lips. It was bulbous, ridged, shaped just perfectly for the job. Groaning deep and low, her body came alive with the introduction of the pulsing shaft.

"This pussy is mine," he growled. "I do with it as I like."

"Oh, Master." Merrie spasmed as he sank in to the hilt. He was treating her like a mere object…a slave, and yet she could not help her body's responses.

"Come for me," he ordered, his hair falling over his forehead. "Show these men that you are mine."

Merrie was awash in shame and hot, fiery need. The orgasm overcame her as he held her fast, his complete and total prisoner. He waited commandingly for it to pass, in concentric waves, building, and looping outward, ever wider, and shallower and then he began to move in pursuit of his own.

"My sweet little copper-haired angel…now it's time…for you to come from a deeper place," he murmured enigmatically.

"No more, please." She didn't think she could take it. She'd taken too much already. Too many sensations, too many atom-shattering explosions, up and down her flesh. Shaking her head, she pleaded with him, "No, stop."

"You are mine," he growled as his semen began to spurt. His face was a delicious mix of intensity and pleasure, his competitiveness transferred from the business field and ball court to this new arena.

Merrie moaned. Using her masturbating fingers, she formed the shape and sensation of that merciless cock, taking and taking and taking. She was chewing on her lips, throwing her head back, converting the dream sequence into a very potent and very real orgasm.

It seemed like hours later Meridian heard the pounding on the office door. Opening her eyes, she looked down between her gaping thighs, the cream slick on her skin. Quickly, guiltily, she snatched away her hand. *I'm losing it*, she thought. *I'm really losing it. I just had sex with myself at my own desk like a horny teenager.*

"It's no use hiding from me, boss," Kennedy called, continuing to tap on the door. "I'm not going away." As always, Meridian's young intern was doing a fine job of not minding her own business.

"Just a minute." Merrie cleaned herself up in the small bathroom adjacent to her paneled office before she finally reconciled herself to the invasion.

She was a little shaky on her feet, the fantasy of being taken by Wilder still half gripping her. It had seemed so real. Had she really done all those things to herself in her imagination? Had she really made this obnoxious, humorless man her Master, even in a fantasy?

"Spill it," demanded the twenty-two year old brunette with the herringbone glasses and hatefully perfect slim body as soon as her boss opened the door. "What's going on?"

Merrie looked at the twin lattes in the cardboard tray in her assistant's left hand. Somehow Kennedy seemed to come up with these out of thin air. In case of emergency, ingest caffeine was her motto.

"In two words or less," replied Merrie grimly. "Marshall Wilder."

Meridian plopped down with her on the leather sofa and proceeded to explain the events of the morning as best she was able, from Wilder's ridiculous treatment of everyone at the meeting to his completely unexpected injunction to her to write a proposal for her own promotion.

Judiciously she left out the sex slave fantasies she was having. Kennedy had enough of a field day with Merrie's lack of regular dates as it was. The last thing Merrie needed was some new outrageous lecture from the young woman on how to fix her sex life. Kennedy's latest idea, which she'd finally talked her out of, had been for her to take a week's holiday at a nudist pleasure colony and single's retreat in the Caribbean.

"But that's good news," Kennedy concluded from her end of the leather couch when Merrie had finished the part about the eight a.m. report. "Isn't it?"

Merrie bit her lip. How could she put it into words?

Kennedy's pretty blue eyes widened. "You do want to be the big *cajuna* around here, don't you?"

"Yeah…yeah, sure I do."

Kennedy wasn't buying it. Cross-legged in her undersized tank top and capri pants, she looked like a postmodern female Buddha, size one.

"Stop looking at me like that," Merrie grumbled. "I've been x-ray-eyed enough for one day."

Kennedy shook her head. "You've really got it bad for him don't you?"

"No," Merrie denied a little too quickly. "I hate him."

"Aha." Kennedy extended her finger, decorated in electric blue polish, the latest trend on the college campus where she spent the other nine months of her life. "Hate is a four letter word—just like love and lust."

"So is nuts," she slurped at the frothy concoction warming her hands. "Which is what you are if you think I have any feelings for that…that man."

Kennedy frowned, indicating that she was not going to let the point go. "I know what this is all about," she said, the wheels in her brain turning dangerously fast. "I should have seen it coming. First Mr. High and Mighty Hot Buns gets here, next thing you know you're all moody. That can only mean one thing."

"PMS?" She asked, hoping to divert her.

Kennedy gave her that maternal look, though she was practically young enough to be Merrie's daughter. "I know about the websites, boss."

"What websites?"

"Do I have to spell it out? Hot babes in collars and chains? Big strapping hunks with leather vests and whips. Anything ring a bell so far?"

Merrie barely avoided spitting out her latte. "Kennedy Erica Fontaine, you have no right looking at my computer!"

Kennedy rolled her eyes like it was Merrie, instead of her, who was totally off-base. "Sheesh. How else am I supposed to be your fairy god-kink-mother?"

"Kennedy, what on earth are you talking about?"

"I'm talking about the answer to all your problems. Don't you see? It's as plain as the drool that comes out of your mouth every time we talk about Wilder."

Merrie threw back her head, in an exasperated appeal to the divinity of the white-washed ceiling. "Is it too late to transfer to the mailroom?" She groaned.

"Yes, it is. Now follow me." Kennedy grabbed her arm, yanking her to her feet.

Merrie was marched to her own desk and made to stand behind her own chair, which in turn was occupied by her young guide. It was the keyboard Kennedy wanted. Merrie watched the blue-tipped fingers fly over the keys, mercilessly digging their way into the Internet in a display of twenty-something surfing that made the older woman's head spin.

"Bingo," she finally concluded, opening her last and final window.

Merrie read the stylized red banner on the black screen of her monitor. "Xchange.com. What does that mean?"

"Your ticket to adventure, bliss and sexual relief. First thing we do is pick a name for you."

"A name?"

"A handle, silly. You know, a sexy alias for online. Something like desprat2Plz. We'll start with that. Nope. Taken," she sighed. "Figures. Hard to be original anymore. How about ownmenow? Cool. That one's still available." She punched a few more buttons. "Okay, you're in. Now remember it, 'cause that's who you'll be whenever you log on."

"And why would I be logging on here exactly?"

"So you can find a Master."

Merrie laughed, hiding the sudden jolt in her stomach. "Okay, now I know you've gone off the deep end."

Kennedy tipped the chair back and twisted her head like the puppy she still was. "Tell me you aren't curious about bondage and domination. Come on, it's written all over your face. Don't be self-conscious. You're not alone. Lots of folks are into it. And it's not what you think, either. No one's gonna ship you off to a slave brothel in Madagascar. All you need is to find a nice dominant gentleman who'll show you the ropes—pardon the expression. Nothing heavy, just a little kinky fun. Some tying, a little flogging. Handcuffs, whatever. You'll get your rocks off, and then you'll have a clear head to deal with the boss man. *Mano a mano*."

"More like I'll be dealing with the unemployment line if word of this gets out."

"It won't. This site is totally discrete. So...what shall we say in your descriptive profile?"

"How about, 'Woman hounded by insane intern looking for one-way trip to deserted island?'"

Kennedy licked her lips, lost in thought. "Sexy redhead," she saw the words in her mind, transferring them instantly onto the screen just like she did when brainstorming for ad campaigns. "Five foot four, one hundred twenty pounds, SWF newbie seeks experienced Dom, r/t, Lt b/d, D/s, ixnay on the 24/7. How does that sound?"

"Like a foreign language."

"We just need a personal quote," Kennedy cheerfully ignored. "Make me your temporary slave, Master, teach me to submit and I promise you won't be sorry. Yes, that's it."

More buttons were punched and the account was fully posted. Merrie felt the sweat collecting on her palms in anticipation of what might come next.

"Good. We're in business, boss. Now all you have to do is sit back and wait for the e-mail to start pouring in."

Merrie took a deep breath. "It might as well be when hell freezes over, Kennedy, because that's how soon I'm going to involve myself in this…this nonsense."

"Don't be silly. We can take some pix for you. Get you a nice, pretty collar to wear and some sexy clothes. That will increase your hits for sure."

Merrie allowed her eyes to roll, though the thought of a collar filled her with wicked, sex-making thoughts. "Sure, Kennedy, whatever you say," she concealed her excitement. "Now would you mind if I did some actual work on my computer?"

"No, problem," she relinquished the seat, oblivious to the sarcasm. "If you want to get an idea of some of the dominant men out there looking for submissive females, you can read profiles this afternoon."

"Exactly how do you know so much about this stuff, anyway, or don't I want to know?"

Kennedy wrinkled her terminally cute, pixie nose. "Good fairy god-kink-mothers never reveal their trade secrets, especially not the self-incriminating ones."

"Yes, I'm sure," Merrie said dryly, resuming her seat and her much neglected workload. Clicking off the website, she steeled herself for a no-nonsense afternoon.

She managed to hold out for all of ten minutes before logging back on to the Xchange to read the profiles. And read. And read.

*****

Marshall Wilder, stripped to T-shirt and slacks, grunted behind the walls of his plush office, mentally counting out his nine hundred and eighty-seventh crunch. Usually exercise calmed him down, but it wasn't working this morning. It was the woman's fault. Meridian Hunter. In just two weeks she had succeeded in aggravating him to an almost unprecedented level. Here it was a half hour past the staff meeting, and he was still in a state of total agitation.

Over the years, he'd faced down cagey Japanese billionaires, stingy Arab princes, not to mention angry charging Bengal tigers on hunting expeditions. Hell, he'd even told Vinny the Nose Nostrano and his extortion boys to take a flying leap and actually gotten away with it. But nothing compared to this compact spitfire—a whirling dervish of red curls, sexy as hell, with a naturally pouting mouth and a complete unwillingness to roll over and play dead.

She ought to be shaking in her pretty little heels, terrified for the loss of her job. And come to think of it, why the hell hadn't he just fired her outright for insubordination? Sure, she was good. Smart and savvy and more than capable of running this company when he moved on, but she was a free thinker and that spelled trouble on a ship as tight as his.

She needed to go. Or at least be made to change her attitude to something more…compliant. Maybe he should just get her to stop wearing those damned tight skirts. Burlap sacks would be a much safer idea.

Switching over to push-ups, he told himself he only kept her on for business reasons, because he didn't want a sex discrimination suit. But there was no denying the raging hard-on that bumped against the maroon carpeted floor with every down-flex of his toned biceps. He'd had this blasted erection the whole time at that meeting, and every time Meridian Hunter opened her luscious, exasperating mouth, it only got worse. Hell, just having her in his vicinity, living and breathing was more than he could take.

He could tell her to start wearing oversized jackets and pants, but what the hell sense did that make? She would be totally right to balk at that one. Anyway, he would only be tipping his hand at how he really felt about her.

She was an employee—he ought to consider her just like all the others. He wasn't entirely heartless. No one seemed to understand that every job he cut was meant to save ten others, maybe the whole company. And by keeping his companies afloat, he kept the economy afloat, and that in turn ensured that the workers he let go had somewhere else to work. It was all a carefully based equation. Subjective emotions could not enter into it.

The whole thing with Meridian was a mess, that's what it was. It was getting personal. And it wasn't just about wanting to take her to bed, either. You'd expect that with a beautiful woman. The average man imagines that with half the women he sees. What Marshall was imagining was far worse, though. To him, the lovely Miss Hunter was a walking advertisement, begging to be dominated. Saucy, with laughing green eyes, wearing her heart on her sleeve, full of bravado one minute, totally docile the next. From the little things she did, licking her lips, fluttering her lashes as she daydreamed, down to how she crossed those long legs, it was all one big provocation—like some schoolgirl poking curiously with a stick in blithe ignorance at the hide of a sleeping lion.

Had she no idea that he had owned females like her in the past—literally? Was there no clue for her at all in his body language and presence that he was a sexual Master and trainer of women? Because as much as he was fighting it, he was playing predator to her prey, already running her down in his mind, imagining her at his mercy, her feminine desires completely ranged against her as he reduced and conquered her. Slowly. Deliciously. Irrevocably.

A woman like that should always be naked before him, her neck and wrists encircled in tight, black leather cuffs, her body trembling with arousal as she knelt in readiness for submission. No longer a mere employer, he would become her Master, taking her to places she had only dared dream of, letting her feel the smack of his hand on her taut buttocks, and the kiss of his paddle or flogger. She would give her body, becoming his treasured possession, whom he'd guard with a ferocity surpassing that of any husband's devotion for his wife.

Damn it, this erection was getting worse. The push-ups he was doing, even the one arm variety, were doing nothing but inciting his blood. He could feel the old temptations creeping in, stronger than ever. What a fool he was. Hadn't he learned anything in the past about going down this road? The game of Master and slave was a thing of the mind, a fantasy. He'd tried once before to live it out—with Jeny—and it had proven an unmitigated disaster. The near ruination of his business and his mental health.

Because of her he'd avoided anything remotely close to a relationship since the divorce. Call girls were fine, though even with them he was careful to keep the sex routine and vanilla. He simply could not afford to stir his deeper urges any longer. Submissive women, those who craved slavery, or at least thought they did, were simply not worth the trouble. They were one of nature's cruel jokes, he'd decided, like the rose that can't be plucked for all the thorns. Or the beautifully colored coral snake with its singularly deadly venom.

What he needed to do right now was masturbate. Get the whole thing out of his system so he could go back to work. Putting his dress shirt back on over his tight white crewneck T-shirt, he headed for the desk. He was harder than he'd been in years. It was like being twenty again—sitting there unzipping his pants to take out his red-hot cock, thickly veined and poking through his boxers.

His fingers were damp and clammy on his uncircumcised shaft. Closing his eyes, he began to stroke himself, squeezing along the vein on the underside, feeling it pulse and throb. A little groan escaped his throat. His balls were tight, full of semen. He was pointing straight and tall, his natural impulse to penetrate a woman at full power level.

Closing his eyes, his cock more iron than flesh, and yet sensitive as any blood-filled thing can be, he tried to conjure the right scene, the right woman. Jenifer came to mind first. The petite blonde fitness instructor who'd begged him to take possession of her body, and than betrayed him with her mind. What an intense, passion-filled relationship that had been. She had called him

Master and meant it, at least when he was inside her, looming over her, or manipulating and torturing her perfect flesh with the whip and flogger and cane. She would scream out her slavery as his cock plunged into her tight depths, that perfect little body covered in sweat, a sacrifice to his sadistic lust. But somehow she was always in control in the end, he going only as far as she wanted, in exactly the right way, with her doing the taking. And still more taking, until finally she had his heart and his bank account to boot.

Beautiful and deadly. His own personal coral snake. He'd tried to help her, truly he had. Like Sir Galahad or one of those ancient knights, he'd ridden in to wipe away her tears and right every wrong in her life. And look where that had gotten him.

Now it was the image of Christine in his romantic clutches, her long dark hair loose about her shoulders. For a thousand dollars an hour, she would make any man's dreams come true. Crawling, begging, surrendering. Lying prostrate on her bed, hands above her head, palms up. The silk of her short negligee strained by her full breasts, silently begging the man to rip the tiny garment from her, letting him know it was included in the price of admission. All while smiling that complicated smile of hers, making all but the most astute of men think there was some glimmer behind those dark eyes, something that would raise it from the mere professional to the personal.

Christine too called him Master. As with Jenifer, it was for money, though at least Christine struck an honest bargain up front. All right, so maybe that wasn't fair. Jenifer had issues, as the psychologists put it. Supposed reasons to justify her ambivalent, heart-stabbing behavior. Wilder smiled at the irony, stripping himself in his fantasy. He would ejaculate inside the pretty prostitute Christine, quickly, efficiently.

As he prepared to take his place, however, the vision abruptly shifted. Christine's face and body blurred, changing into that of another. Meridian. Red hair fanned out on the silk pillows in place of Christine's black. Wide green eyes, in place of the other's darkly swirling blue ones.

He could see her, as clear as day, the image burned into his brain, overtaking him as surely as any reality, her perplexing beauty, her full, enticing lips, always on the verge of a smile...complex and seductive. And that body, what must that body look like under her clothes and what wouldn't he give to see it, to have her squirming helplessly in his arms, completely under his power.

Marshall stopped his stroking. He did not like the direction this was taking. Suddenly it was more like the fantasy was having him and not the other way around.

No, this simply wouldn't do. It was as good as giving in to the woman by admitting she had the power to get to him. And what was he going to do—jerk off after every staff meeting, not to mention all the other times he saw her, sauntering down the hall, standing at the water cooler, or, god forbid, bending down for a dropped pencil?

Talk about things getting out of hand. He had actually wanted to spank Meridian's bottom during the meeting. It was all he could think about, actually. Dragging her across his lap, flipping up her skirt and swatting those sweet little panty-covered cheeks. He wanted that power.

Hell, he wanted that right, signed over by her. Ironclad, giving him *carte blanche* to ignore her whines and protests and put her back in line, back where she knew she wanted to be, even though she was fighting it, and always would. Though she would never, ever fail to thank him afterward.

It was the endless tug of war with obedience. Her high-spirited mind battling with her sex, with him as the beneficiary each and every time. It was a tempting, pretty picture indeed. Meridian Hunter represented the full package. Beauty, brains and the natural vibes of a submissive. Without realizing it, she carried herself as if on display to potential Masters. Showing herself, making it clear that, for the right man she would do anything at all. Give everything.

Marshall Wilder put away his cock, still pulsing and aching with need. Desperate times call for desperate measures, he thought, logging himself onto the site he hadn't been to in nearly two and a half years. Since he'd met Jenifer.

Xchange.com. Where the jaded meet the clueless.

Marshall licked his dry lips. He wasn't exactly sure what good would come of it, except that he would regain his perspective on things. His employees deserved a better boss, one with a level head, one not driven by uncontrolled fantasies. Sure, he wouldn't actually fulfill those fantasies online, but he would be able to drum the hard truth into his head—again—that there were no realities behind these old sex dreams and the sooner he saw them for what they were and extinguished them, the better for everyone.

Especially Meridian.

Chapter Two

"Kennedy, this is absolutely, positively not going to work," called out a naked Meridian from inside her bedroom.

"How do you know if you won't even come here and try?" argued the young woman from the other side of the door.

Merrie hated the logic. Almost as much as she hated the clothes—or lack thereof—she was supposed to model for the website pix, leather cuffs and collar, a black leather corset, a lacy black G-string and…nothing else.

"I just want to go back to being sexually frustrated," she cried out. "I want to go home… I just want ice cream and fudge and I want—"

"Want what?" Challenged Kennedy. "To become the youngest spinster on the planet? You know you're not meant for that. Take a chance. For me. For yourself."

Merrie gulped, looking at the items on her bed. What she wanted was for some man—him, damn it—to make her put them on, to not tolerate her silly female squeamishness and just make it an order.

The idea of having no choice made her wet. Almost as wet as staring at this scandalous attire Kennedy had somehow scrounged up for her with only a few hours advance notice. Kennedy had promised no face shots, just her body. As if that would make her feel any better about being exposed to the world as a sex fiend.

A bastard like Marshall Wilder would probably love a sight like this, seeing her so exposed and intimidated. The man had no respect for women, obviously. He ordered Sharon around like a dog, expecting her to be at his beck and call every minute of the day. And he obviously hated it whenever Merrie tried to speak up in Sharon's or anyone else's defense. She'd seen, or thought she had, the intensity behind his eyes just today as she'd dared to question him when he'd told Avery to stay late producing a report that could easily wait until tomorrow.

Yes, she was quite sure Mr. Male Chauvinist Pig Boss would be thrilled to put her in her place like this. She could imagine the man calling her into his office, these very cuffs, collar, and negligee on his desk.

"Put them on, Miss Hunter, and we'll have a little chat."

Always Miss Hunter, said with such condescension. Like she was a little girl. She hated it, but what would she do if he pushed that hard? Would she obey and strip for him or would she tell him to go to hell, no matter how good a job she might be passing up?

Merrie fingered the thin leather collar. It was black with diamond studs on it. Harsh, yet pretty in its own way. She held it up to the soft light of her bedside lamp. Was she really going to advertise herself this way to thousands of men? Would she really put it on and let Kennedy take pictures? It was a ghastly notion, but still, it was better than ever showing it to Wilder.

Grimly, she fastened it on. The touch of the leather to her skin quickened her heart, just a little. Its symbolism was very powerful. A woman who wore this belonged to someone. She was owned. What would that mean? In bed? Or out of it?

Merrie's lips were dry. She licked them. What next? The cuffs. These were leather, too, with metal clasps and tiny padlocks. Each padlock had a key still in it, though if a man—a Master—were to put them on he'd hold the keys himself. Or else what would be the point of locking a female up? The cuffs weren't meant for her—the slave girl—to take off. They were for restraint. Control. And probably for sexual use, as well.

She fastened them snugly. They felt good, reassuring, although she wasn't sure why. Up close she noticed each cuff had a small metal ring on it, with a spring opening. You could attach them together with the rings. Behind the prisoner's back or in front. Her lips kept getting dry. She licked them again.

Possibilities flashed through her mind. Ways a slave could be restrained. Helpless. Open. Sexually available.

Shifting her thighs, she noticed the wetness. Some fashion show this was going to be. She went for the corset next. A somber looking thing, more an instrument of torture than a proper garment. It was hard to believe, once upon a time, that all women wore these. Then again, there was also a time when every woman, even a high-placed wife, was someone's possession.

Was there a correlation, she wondered, between the bondage-like garment and the status of its wearers in history?

Merrie put it aside for the moment. The corset was going to require Kennedy's help. She went for the G-string instead, slipping it over her dainty, bare feet and pulling it up her legs and thighs and over her mound. Her sopping-wet mound.

For some reason it only now dawned on her that the corset wouldn't cover her breasts. It would be worse than being nude.

"Go home, Kennedy, I'm serious, I changed my mind," she announced with as much fortitude as possible. "I'm not going through with this."

"No way, kiddo. I'm camping outside this door 'til you let me in. And I'm ordering a dozen pizzas on your credit card and pay-per-views every hour on your TV 'til you come out."

Merrie padded to the door. Her bare feet tingled on the carpet as she walked. For some reason it felt strange to be upright as opposed to crawling. "That's blackmail," she unlocked the door.

"All's fair," Kennedy burst in. "In love and kink."

Her assistant snatched up the corset. "This is going to be so hot. Go sit over there at your vanity, we'll get this on you."

Meridian did as she was told. The face in the mirror looked back at her uncertainly. *Don't look at me,* she told herself. *I haven't a clue what I'm doing either.*

But she did have an idea what she was doing. And why. Several ideas in fact. Her erect nipples being two. Proof-positive, along with her pulsing, greedy sex that this whole business of dressing for potential Masters was turning her on. More so than any of the actual sex she'd ever had in her life, as a matter fact. The thought boggled her mind. How could it be that a mere game of pretend all by her lonesome could surpass the intensity of all the human loving she'd known? What kind of woman did that make her? Not a very normal one, she was afraid.

"Kennedy, you're sure this will work? I mean what if I don't even get any responses to my profile at all?"

"Honey, you'll need to hire somebody full-time just to screen them all for you. Trust me, you've got it—the words, the look, the whole deal. Your only problem is going to be choosing."

"But I don't want to be anyone's slave, temporary or not," she said, not very convincingly.

"Don't worry, we won't let anyone chain you to their stove all day long cooking fritters and baked beans, or whatever else it is people do with stoves. Just a few one-night stands to knock your stockings off, and you can say *sayonara* to whichever dude you end up going with."

"I should be writing my proposal for Wilder," she said.

"That'll keep 'til later."

"But it has to be perfect. You know how he is. I don't want any slip-ups."

Kennedy eyed Merrie's reflection. "And you don't want to be this man's slave, huh? Seems to me Wilder has you on a short leash already."

"What's that supposed to mean? I'm professional and thorough in my work. That's all."

"Chill, boss," she patted Merrie's shoulder. "Didn't mean to hit a nerve."

"Well you didn't," she snapped. "I just want the promotion, that's all."

"Sure you do," Kennedy said yanking on the corset strings. "Sure you do."

* * * * *

Marshall was still in his office at half past twelve. He'd been hammering out orders for the Nikkei in Tokyo, and now he was waiting for the exchange to open in London. He was in a worse mood than this morning, if that was possible. The walls were definitely starting to close in on him. Running this advertising business was getting to him. Too bloody small. If his doctors hadn't advised him to do something about his blood pressure, he would never have stooped to personally managing one of his nickel and dime companies.

Technically, he was supposed to be on vacation, kicking back on some tropical island, barefoot in a hammock with a Mai Tai. Well this was as close as it got to relaxation for Marshall Trenton Wilder, consummate overachiever and son of a longshoreman from Philadelphia. Rubbing his eyes, he contemplated his next move. He could bed down on the couch, catch forty minutes or so then get back up for the night. Or else go back to his hotel suite and stare at the gilded walls.

He decided to check the website again. Putting himself back in circulation as a practicing Master looking for a slave was one of his more outlandish moves in quite some time. Right up there with the urban parachuting phase he went through last year.

Not that he was worried about finding anyone. Filling out a new profile, he'd told himself nothing would come of it and it would just confirm what he already knew, that BDSM desires could only get you hurt. It was going to be a lesson for himself. An exercise in futility done for a reason. If anyone thought Marshall Wilder was hard on his employees, they had no clue how he drove himself. Or punished himself.

Not that he cared what people thought. His treatment of his subordinates was for their own good. Survival was the name of the game in this life and those who learned that prospered while those who didn't stayed poor. And ignorant.

Like the rest of Marshall's family. Some people couldn't be helped. He'd learned that the hard way. Sometimes the best you could do was move on, try and make something of yourself, thereby creating a decent climate for others to thrive in.

He saw a lot of himself in Meridian. She had come up from the bottom, too, as he'd understood it. It had sounded like he was lecturing her, sharing his story about the ditches, but really he was trying to connect, just a little. And maybe that's why he was tough on her, too. Because that's what made strong people stronger.

Not surprisingly, Marshall saw no one of interest among the pool of eligible females on the Xchange.com database. Just as he'd observed in the past, on the surface there seemed to be thousands to choose from, but when you culled it down for age, location, education level and so on, you were inevitably left with a tired handful, all of them easily divided into a few categories, each deadly in their own way.

First, were the huntresses. Young women looking for mates. Rich ones, preferably. There was no limit to what a woman would do to find a wealthy husband, including crawling and posing naked with a whip between her teeth. As far as Marshall was concerned, such women gave submissives a bad name. A truly submissive woman had to want to surrender for her own reasons. She had to need it—no matter what the cost.

Then came the teases. Pretty bodies wanting to play with the heads of egomaniacal Dominants with low IQs. Come and dominate me…if you can. Jump through my hoops—always one more—and I'll be your pleasure slave, forever. Any Dominant with experience knew this for the ridiculous joke it was. Real slaves came with real histories and any Master worth his salt can tell you up front what the slave's problems are going to be, and you can be sure they all have some. There's no such thing as a fantasy come true—that's what Marshall had learned.

Finally there were the just plain clueless types, women who didn't know why they were there or what they were really asking for. They weren't submissives, just pretenders, albeit innocent ones. At first, he'd taken Jenifer for one of these.

He'd met her at a gathering of the Damien Society, a very ancient and revered group of sado-masochists in New York. She had a master's in psychology and a penchant for pain. What he would not find out until after marriage, however, was that her masochism was bottomless, her very soul seeking out and sucking in energy, which in turn would be spit out in terrible, vomited storms.

Jenifer was of that very special breed of submissives, the split personality. On the one hand, constantly demanding abuse, while on the other, plotting her man's destruction from the beginning. You had to be involved with one of this type to appreciate the truly hellish delusions you could sink into together. Of course, that didn't mean she was stupid. Especially when it came time to hire attorneys to work out the divorce.

Marshall logged on to his account and clicked onto the new members section, with the recently added photos.

Photos told a lot, and more than just about the person's body. They told about the heart, the mind. Three more sets had been uploaded tonight, close enough to match his home area. The first two held no interest. The third he surveyed just because the young woman was good to look at. She was reclined on a bed. Wearing a black G-string, her slender hand resting on a long leg. She wore pink nail polish. His eyes traveled up her torso. He could make out the bottom of her chin and the color of her hair, wild and loose about her ears.

It was deep red. Copper-red. Crimson, spun and sparkling. A real looker. Definitely a tease. A poser, wanting some free praise from men, fools who would line up to tell her how they wanted to chain her to their beds and whip her. A bunch of lunatic Tarzans, never knowing she was on the other end of the camera laughing her pretty little behind off.

Just for the hell of it, he checked out her other pictures. The second one had her sitting up, holding her naked breasts, the nipples erect, vulnerable. She had cuffs on and it was hard not to automatically imagine snapping them together and putting her through her paces. Exactly what the little tart wants, he thought, a man fool enough to believe he can be the one to turn this wet dream into reality.

In the third picture she posed with her hands over her head. It showed her from the forehead up, tiny worry lines above her expressive eyebrows, and her palms turned up, in a very innocent almost sweet way. Something about it struck him. A little different maybe? Not so preprogrammed? And why did this woman seem familiar?

He clicked onto her profile. She was a beginner, no practical experience. She lived in the city, less than five miles from his locale according to the databank. Single. No listing for age, though she didn't look much past thirty. ownmenow was her screen name. Corny. Typical newbie stuff. At least she wasn't some New Age fruit loop, though. The fruit loops had names like "asherahmoon," or "draculagirl" and quoted whole paragraphs of *The Prophet* by Gibran without understanding a word. They told you how they liked to eat sushi at midnight on the roof while listening to Wagner.

The woman could only be a poser. Though the quote didn't quite fit.

"Make me your temporary slave, Master, teach me to submit and I promise you won't be sorry."

It was relatively humble, and actually showed a little understanding of and willingness to play the game. Going back to the pictures, he hit maximize. What the hell was it about this woman that was making him look twice? The body was nice, very nice, but frankly, he could get women this good at the drop of a hat.

Maybe it was the hair. Who did he know with hair like that?

Or was it that ring on her finger? Yes, that was it. He'd seen it before. And recently, too. Plain silver, hammered and inlaid with Indian turquoise. Distinctive. Unusual.

Wilder's jaw tensed as it came to him. He'd seen that very ring today or else a dead ringer for it. Could it be the same—the jewelry and the female both? Quickly, he looked for something else in the profile to rule out the possibility. She had red hair. That fit. The location. That was right. Single, white, female. Five foot four. A hundred and twenty pounds.

Sonofabitch.

Emotions raced through Marshall now, ones he'd hoped would never come again. There was anger, confusion, and a sense of deep, deep worry for this female he hardly knew. If he wasn't careful he would be pulling out that old armor, trying to play knight again to her damsel in distress.

If this really was Meridian Hunter, then she was making a choice with her life, and he couldn't protect her, even if it was a bad choice. She'd get hurt on the net. Hurt bad. He could only hope it wasn't her, that she would listen to reason. Women, pretty, young women like her should be looking for mates at church socials, not online.

He checked his watch. One thirty. Six and a half hours until Meridian Hunter's report was due. Good. He'd be waiting for her. With a few questions. Not to mention a little surreptitious jewelry inspection.

*****

Merrie was an absolute total mess by the time she got to Wilder's office. It was ten after eight and she was flush, eyes puffy from a night of no sleep, her heart racing about as fast as a fox with a pack of hounds nipping at its heels.

Speaking of heels, she had mismatched hers. One blue. One black. How frazzled could one female human being get in anticipation of encountering a male? she wondered bleakly. It didn't help that she'd been reading her Xchange.com e-mails until six in the morning, pouring over all those men from all over the world who were interested in her. Little Meridian Hunter from Lexview,

Ohio, graduate of Ohio Central College and the Manhattan School of Business.

And they all wanted to play Master to her slave. To ownmenow, the ridiculous character she was supposed to be with her studded collar, sexy corset and leather cuffs. To her it had seemed a little over the top, but apparently the effect was very real—on her and the men. She could hardly keep herself dry, in fact, at the thought of them all wanting her, craving to put her body into bondage, to use her as their love toy.

And my goodness, weren't some of them forward, too. Quite a number had told her in no uncertain terms what would happen to her and how she would respond to them sexually in their clutches. Twice she'd had to stop and masturbate just thinking of those strong hands controlling her, making her perform and dance and give of her deepest desires.

The funny thing was, no matter how good they talked or looked—and there were some real cuties—she kept coming back to one thing, how they stacked up against Wilder. A very few were as handsome, or nearly so, but they had fallen woefully short in charisma, or bravado. A few seemed cocksure, but she could just picture Marshall wiping up the floor with them, with barely a motion of his eyebrow. All of which was crazy, because she didn't even like the man much less want to ever be with him.

Bottom line, she was going to have to pick somebody and just give it a try. Being alone was driving her crazy. She couldn't keep masturbating constantly. And she couldn't afford to lose many more nights' sleep either, or she'd lose her job.

The report for Wilder never did get finished last night. Thankfully she'd been thinking about this plan to run the company for so long that it had spilled out of her in twenty minutes flat this morning. A quick spell check on the document and she was good to go.

Except for the shoes.

And the dress. That worried her a little, too. It was mid-calf length, very unslinky and made of nice, conservative cotton. It could pass for church, but was it professional enough? *Not to worry,* she thought glumly, *he'll be too busy looking at my feet and trying to decide if I should be sent back to kindergarten for a refresher course in color selection.*

A final adjustment to her hair, which she'd decided to keep down and loose, and Meridian was knocking on his office door.

"Who is it?" came his deep, raspy voice, sexy as sin. Already she could feel the butterflies fluttering in her stomach, a whole new species she swore could be named just for him.

"It's Meri—It's Miss Hunter, sir."

"Come in," he barked as though she were coming uninvited just to annoy him and not as a result of his direct instructions.

Naturally he wanted her off-balance again. What was it about him that had to be so totally in control all the time? And why did she have to be so darned fascinated with him when he acted that way?

"Mr. Wilder, I'm sorry I'm late." She presented herself and the report before the imposing mahogany desk. "I was—"

"Put it on the credenza," he cut her off. "And have a seat."

This time he wanted her in one of the wingbacks facing the aircraft carrier-sized surface. He'd had the desk flown in when he took over. Pure excess, in her opinion. Then again, the man wasn't only owner of this company, but a dozen more, all under a corporate umbrella that made him darned close to a billionaire. Many had wondered at his coming here to manage this place, tiny as it was. Some said it had something to do with his mental state after his failed marriage. Whatever it was, he didn't seem real fragile to her.

She supposed she shouldn't care, but there was a part of her that wondered, maybe even worried, just a bit. He looked tired this morning, showing his age a little. There were slight lines under his eyes, and the tiniest crow's feet. She doubted he'd slept much. Some nights he never even left the building, according to the night custodians.

"Are you happy working here, Miss Hunter?" He asked from his throne-like seat.

Merrie tried not to squirm at the jarring, unexpected inquiry. She took a moment to size him up. The man had on a navy blue suit today and a light blue shirt, designed to bring out his vivid, probing eyes. He'd matched it with a red tie, white specked, the pattern too small to make out. His hair was freshly combed and he smelled of musk.

Idly, she thought of running her fingers through his hair, of being the first to see him dressed in the morning. *Darling, you look wonderful today,* she would say, and he would hold her and tell her she was beautiful.

"I've put five years of my life into this place, Mr. Wilder," she replied, trying simultaneously to hide her shoes and her expression.

His lips curled into a slight frown. She was starting to memorize those little expressions of his. He had a thousand. Sometimes she would dream them, wondering what it would feel like to touch each one, tracing the line of his lips, across his dimples.

"That's not an answer, Miss Hunter."

His tone shifted, breaking her reverie. For some reason, this tripped her off, causing her to speak her mind with uncharacteristic bluntness. It was hard to say if she was just overtired, or if for some reason she trusted that she could go as far as she wanted with this man because she knew he would keep it all under control. Including her. "Sir, with all due respect, my happiness is not at issue. And if it's my job performance that concerns you, I'm sure you know how to fire me. You've done enough of it around here already."

She braced herself for a firestorm, but the great Marshall Wilder remained placid, studying her, waiting for her next move. He reminded her of one of those chess champions, or a great general surveying a battlefield. Except whatever the rules of engagement were, he alone knew them.

Merrie decided she'd had enough mind games. "If you're not interested in my proposal, *sir,* I will be going. To pack my desk."

"I'm more interested in your ring, Miss Hunter."

"My what?"

He inclined his head, cool, imperious. "That ring on your finger. Where did you get it?"

"New Mexico," she replied, though she really ought to have told him it was none of his goddamned business.

"It's Native American, isn't it? Turquoise? Did your boyfriend buy it for you, or weren't you seeing anyone at the time?"

Merrie felt the blood pour into her face. "Mr. Wilder have you any idea how vastly inappropriate that question is?"

"So sue me," he shrugged. "Even my lawyers have lawyers. With any luck, your granddaughter will get a nice chunk of my estate—which by that time will be stuck in probate or turned over to one of my deadbeat nephews, anyway."

His eyes were flashing, sending something in his own personal Morse code, like a lighthouse in the midst of a storm, only she didn't understand his language and at this stage of the game, she didn't care to learn it either.

"Sir, I have no idea what this is all about. But this conversation is over." She was on her feet, concentrating on putting them one in front of the other. With any luck she'd make it to the door without passing out.

"Miss Hunter, one more thing."

Merrie's hand clenched the doorknob. What was it with this man stopping her at the door all the time? "Mr. Wilder, I don't think there's anything more to say."

"The hell there isn't. One month from today you're taking over. Forget the proposal, I want concrete plans by Thursday. With complete estimates of how much extra money you're going to line my pockets with this year in increased profits. Is that clear?"

"Sir?"

He squared his jaw, proud, defiant, more masculine than ever. "Don't answer a question with a question. Are you taking the job or not? I'll give you two and a half times your salary and stock options for Wilder Industries."

Merrie's mouth was unable to close. At some point she mumbled "yes" and closed the door behind her. Hands trembling, she pulled her cell phone out of her purse. Kennedy was just leaving her apartment, on her way to the office.

"What's up, boss?"

"Lattes," she managed to say. "And make them doubles."

* * * * *

Meridian was ownmenow. Wilder was certain of it. The ring would have been proof enough, but there was no mistaking the hair, either, upon closer examination. And her whole demeanor was a dead giveaway. Yesterday she was stiff, awkward, and today she had that whole curious wannabe bondage kitten thing going for her. Getting on the site was working her up. No doubt some boyfriend had tied her up in college, and she'd gotten nostalgic. Or whatever other lame reason this seemingly sane woman had for putting herself on a meat market like the Xchange. Had she no idea what those men were like? At the very least she was going to be emotionally bruised, and god forbid she ever go somewhere to meet some strange man for kinky sex. She was liable to wind up a statistic. He'd had way too many firsthand experiences of pseudodominant men who were nothing more than bullies and abusers. They found their perfect victims in well-meaning submissive females with deep-seated needs to obey and yield to powerful males.

Jenifer had been involved with one when they'd met. He'd had to tell him rather politely but firmly that his presence was no longer desired in her life or in the BDSM community as a whole. It had taken a short but rather one-sided physical encounter to convince the man.

Nothing made Marshall angrier than seeing a man exploit a woman that way. But what could he do when women went after them of their own accord—even ones as well educated and savvy as Meridian?

He'd been halfway tempted to confront her on the spot. Likely she'd just get embarrassed, though and deny the whole thing. He'd have to sort through a mountain of female obfuscation and in the end she wouldn't believe his warnings, anyway. These newbies with stars in their eyes never did.

There was only one solution. It was unorthodox and a bit bizarre, but, in his opinion, it was quite necessary if he intended to save his soon to be managing vice president. What he was going to have to do was to beat her at her own game. Sitting himself at the keyboard, he started thinking out his opening gambit. Miss Meridian Hunter was in for a wake-up call—an embarrassing lesson that might well save her life.

Punching up the response key to her profile, he began an introductory e-mail using his own guise as an online Master. "Dear ownmenow, I can tell from your profile that you are not like the others," he typed. "I have read your profile and I am considering your offer of yourself…"

The rest poured out of him, fast and slick, good dominant talk, just the sort of thing romantic, submissive females fell for like a ton of lead. Lying for a cause, that's what it was. He would make her fall for an invented Internet character, set up an eventual meeting and then she'd see how easy it was to be deceived and how utterly foolhardy it was to trust your body or your heart to a fantasy. Especially in BDSM.

Yes, he would make her hard and brittle. Like himself. No one would ever hurt her. She would be spared every pain he could protect her from. She would be an island. A successful, rich island.

And one day she would thank him for it.

The best part is that he would accomplish all this without being her knight in shining armor. No, that he would not do. As lovely and intriguing as she might be, as charming and irresistible in whatever medieval gown would go with his shiny metal suit, he would not fall into that trap. Not in a million years. Even if it meant shutting his heart off forever. To every other being on the planet, male and female.

For her own good, he repeated to himself. *I will make her an island, just like me.*

Chapter Three

Merrie could hardly concentrate. All she could think of as she listened to the creative team's pitch for the new Sea Mist Hair products line was him. Make that Him, with a capital H. Master Nightshade, her cool, sweet cyber-seducer who'd managed in just four short days to open her heart and mind to vistas of sexual feeling she'd never known existed. Without even seeing his face or hearing his voice on the phone it was like she knew him, and he her. He could almost read her mind. Getting inside it, to all the deep and steamy places, the places you didn't speak about, even to your close friends.

He knew how to please her, by making her please him. He could take her, in so many ways, transporting her each night to some new exotic locale where he would woo her and win her all over again. She'd worn his chains in a warrior's ancient castle, sailed with him down the Grand Canal of Venice in a gondola under moonlight, and even blasted with him into space, to a galaxy where women were slaves and men were ruthless exploiters of their soft, vulnerable flesh.

No man had ever known her inside and out like this. Her orgasms under his electronic tutelage were the best of her life. The hottest and the longest. And the richest, too.

The most amazing thing of all was that she wasn't thinking and dreaming of Marshall Wilder. Yes, she had to face him at work, but he was strangely absent in her fantasies. It was a curious loss, but her new Master kept her from looking too deeply into the reason for things. He wanted her feeling and not thinking. He wanted her in a whirlwind, a constant, delicious daze.

And now he wanted to meet her. The thought thrilled her, but, oh, god, was she ready? She could ask Kennedy. But what would she know? The first president she was old enough to remember was Clinton. There was no way she was qualified to give out love advice. Which is precisely why she'd kept her relationship with Master Nightshade a secret.

If this could be called a relationship. Sure, she spent hours talking to him online every night, chatting about all kinds of things, from silly childhood stories to the best places to stay in Madrid on a budget. Sure, he made her heart sing and she would get wet just seeing that she'd gotten a message from him in her inbox. In every way it was like he was there with her. And when he told her to masturbate, it might as well have been his fingers inside her, and not her own. The way he commanded her and made her feel things more strongly, more intimately than any lover she'd ever known.

Was she ready to meet him? In one way, she already knew him. At least she thought she did. What would it be like in person, though, seeing and interacting for real? It could be disappointing, even disastrous. A sudden case of cold feet overcame her at the prospect. She'd never be able to go through with it. It was a fantasy. A dream. That was all. She had to get a grip. Start taking back control of her life from this stranger before it was too late.

"No more," she called out, not realizing she'd said the words aloud.

"Boss?" Kennedy was looking at her from across the table, head cocked.

"Bad idea, right?" Said Harrison sheepishly as he stood in front of the easel with his mockup magazine ad, the board covered with a medley of dancing shampoo bubbles.

"No...it's not that." She was on her feet. "I just need...some air."

Trying not to run, she made it back to her office. Her plan was to tell him no, not in a million years. But as she found her way to the website, something else kicked in. A deeper feeling—her own, and yet not her own. Almost as if they belonged to someone else, she watched her fingers pecking out the reply e-mail. A minute later she was punching the button to send her message.

There. It was set in stone now. Too late to change. A feeling of panic set in, followed by a strange sense of calm. She'd actually done it. And now the ball was in his court.

Her heart fluttered as she imagined her Master reading the short but sweet e-mail—*Am ready. Tell me where to be, and when.*

Would he know she was only bluffing and let her off the hook, or would he really tell her to be somewhere, at some specific place and time to enact the fantasies they'd both been licking their lips over?

Telling herself she didn't care, she hunkered down into the seat. To wait.

*****

Marshall shook his head as he read the message. So she was actually ready to meet him after less than a hundred hours interaction. The naïve little fool. Obviously this was good in one way, as it would allow him to prove his point and settle the matter relatively quickly. In another way, though, it was disheartening. He'd half hoped she'd be too smart to fall into his trap.

He had to admit, too, he wasn't so anxious to end their little charade. The fact was, Meridian—who ought to have been called prey, not hunter—was an intelligent woman, quick-witted. Precisely the kind of woman a strong, domineering man wishes to command and own.

She was bright and funny. And sexy as hell. A million times more so in the wide open, yet secure forum of the Internet, than she was in person. It was a good thing he was doing this merely as an exercise, lest he actually develop some misplaced feelings for her. The whole point, though, was for him to look like someone pretending to be interested in her, so he could prove that the wrong man, setting her up, lying to her, could cause her to wind up dead.

She was way too trusting for her own good. She ought to be laying down stipulations, specifying that they meet in a public place, of her choosing, where she could have a built-in safety check to call a girlfriend. Instead, she was lost in fantasyland. Wanting to be swept off her feet by some romantic Prince Charming.

He jotted off a quick instant message, to see if she was online.

Sure enough, she came bounding to his side, his little cybernetic lamb.

Master... Sir, I'm so happy to see you. Yes, yes, of course, I will see you...

The Fortin Hotel, he typed. *Tonight at eight. At the front desk, announce yourself as Mrs. Gray. Ask for your room key.*

Here was the real test. He sat back to wait.

Oh, yes, Master. What shall I wear?

Marshall frowned. She'd failed the make-up exam big-time. Agreeing to meet a stranger in a hotel room of all places? It didn't get much more foolhardy than that. *Wear red. No panties,* he wrote outlandishly. *And no one must know where you are. Leave your cell phone in the car.*

I will obey, Master.

He clenched his fists, a storm of emotions surging through him. He logged off with a curt, *That will be all.*

He had way too much on his mind to carry on one of their chats right now. The fact that she really was as foolish as he'd feared was only half the problem. The other half had to do with the fallout of what he'd been doing to her, and, even worse, how she was making him feel.

Light and springy. Laughter-filled. Energized. Attached. All the dread warning signs of the Disease. Incipient attachment. Creeping relationshipitis. The false illusion, the great killer and backstabber called love, rendered ten times as deadly in its Master and slave form. He'd been down that road before and he knew well where it led. To divorce court, to be precise, to have your clock cleaned, the stars still in your eyes as your supposedly devoted, submissive little wife tells, with tears in her eyes, of the mental cruelty she's been made to endure from her brute of a husband.

Wilder ground his teeth. This whole thing was getting way too personal, just like he'd said from the start. He was trying to make something good out of this, like he always did, but he wasn't sure he was being so objective anymore. That was the problem with always being the one in command. You had to see what needed to be done before anyone else, and then you had to act, and sometimes you had to do so without complete information.

In Merrie's case, he'd made a decision and there would be an outcome, way more positive overall than negative. Still, the sooner this gruesome little lesson was over, the better. As soon as possible afterward, he intended to be moving on. Out of this company. And even this city for a while. And most certainly out of the life of the tempestuous, contradiction-filled Meridian Hunter.

* * * * *

Merrie stood outside the elevator, the corridor wall holding her up. There was no telling how big a mistake she was about to make. Every ounce of her reason and her self-preservation instinct told her she shouldn't be doing this. What if Master Nightshade was a psycho or an axe murderer? But he didn't act like one, she told herself. It was like he knew her. They had fun together, and he could make her laugh and feel so many things that she'd long since given up on ever having in life.

How could all that be wrong? It couldn't, which is why she'd come to the Fortin Hotel in the red dress, with the red bra and red shoes. And yet here she was, trembling in the hallway, building up her courage to go to his room. She hoped she was pretty enough. Her hair was swept up in a style she hoped would please him. She had left work early just to get ready.

Kennedy knew something was up, but Merrie was determined not to let the young woman in on it. After all, she had her Master's orders. Besides, this was her business. Her life.

Meridian gulped hard. Was this man really willing to be *her* Master, to teach her and treasure her and dominate her? Only one way to find out. Teetering on shaking legs, she made her way down the hall. Pictures stared thoughtlessly from the papered walls while the room numbers climbed with their quiet, indisputable logic on the identical rows of doors. Fourteen-twelve. Fourteen-fourteen. Fourteen-sixteen.

Fourteen-eighteen. The butterflies she'd been fighting all day turned a particularly energetic somersault in her tummy. This was it. The moment of truth. The moment of decision. With a numb hand, feeling nearly paralyzed, she knocked. Timid. Light, the sound barely audible.

"Come in," she heard the man say.

It was a command not a request. The knob was cold to the touch. The metal became immediately slippery with her sweat. She turned it, releasing the lock. "Hello?"

He was waiting for her, sitting in an armchair facing the door. Stone faced, impassive. Eyes glittering.

"Mr. Wil—" The rest of his name choked in the back of her throat.

How had he found out? More to the point, what kind of trouble was she going to be in for doing this? If indeed she could be faulted for being kinky on her own time.

"Close the door, Miss Hunter."

She did so, bracing herself against it. "I hadn't...expected you."

"Of course you hadn't." He was supremely irritated, fingers gripping the armrest. She noted he'd changed his clothes. In place of his suit he wore a green polo shirt and a pair of khakis. Less a boss now, he seemed even more a man. A sexy, very intimidating one at that

"You were expecting a different man, obviously. Someone you've never met."

She cocked her head. This was growing more curious by the moment. Could the man really have some clue what she was up to? "I'm here to meet my Aunt Matilda," she attempted to cover herself.

"Really? Care to furnish some proof?"

Merrie stiffened. "Sir, my private life is...is private and I'll thank you to stay out of it."

"Apparently it's quite open on Xchange.com, though, isn't it?"

The room began to spin.

"I know what you've been doing there," Wilder accused, his eyes more black now than blue. "I know all about your Master Nightshade. More than anyone else in the world, as a matter of fact. Have you any idea how easy it is to manufacture an identity, Miss Hunter? To throw out a few salient details, a few innuendos to hook an unsuspecting woman?"

"I'm not sure what you're insinuating, but Master Nightshade is very real, I promise you, and when he comes here, he will surely defend my honor," Meridian insisted quite irrationally.

The Wilder brow furrowed. "Don't make it worse by denying the reality, Miss Hunter. The only one you are fooling is yourself. You don't want to look at the mess you've gotten yourself into. Well, you'll have to face the music, now, and you'll thank me for it in the morning. I am Master Nightshade and I have completely deceived you. As could have any nefarious character in my place."

The tears were pooling in her eyes, but she held herself rigid and dignified. She wanted to crawl into a hole and die, but she was not going to give this man any kind of victory. Not now, not here.

"It's a lesson, Miss Hunter," she heard him say without the slightest bit of human warmth. "We all get them in life. You have only one choice. Buck up, go home and get a good night's sleep. Tomorrow we'll discuss your plans for assuming operational management."

Merrie shook her head. There was so much she didn't know at this point—including who she was or where her life was going. But she did know one thing. This arrogant bastard, handsome as he was, had gone too far. He'd stepped over the line.

"No," she choked. "We won't be discussing anything tomorrow, Mr. Wilder. Because I quit!"

"Miss Hunter, this is not acceptable," he said gruffly. "You may not leave in this fashion."

"Go to hell," replied Meridian, not bothering to close the door behind her. *Must hold it together*, she thought as she made a beeline for the elevator. *Must look normal and happy until I get home. Until I can barricade my miserable self in my miserable apartment. Forever.*

*****

Marshall Wilder continued to stare at the opened door for quite some time. To say his little lesson with Miss Hunter had not gone according to plan would be something of an understatement. More accurately, it had been an unmitigated disaster. She hadn't responded at all reasonably.

His fingers played over the armrests of the chair as he contemplated his next move. Should he respond to her whirlwind performance? She'd told him off, she'd quit, she'd run off. That was her loss. Anyone could be replaced—even him. This small company was already taking up way too much of his time. He didn't need this kind of drama.

Hadn't the woman looked incredible in red, though? The sight of her had taken his breath away, with her fiery tresses upswept, and her curvaceous body teasingly hugged by the silky dress. And what a pair of legs under those stockings. Far more provocative than they'd ever looked in the office. He'd had a hard-on the minute he saw her. Hardly in keeping with the professional, told-you-so attitude he had assumed with regard to the whole affair.

It was a dangerous game he'd been playing with this woman, and he was glad it was over. Both the Internet relationship, and the cat and mouse affair they'd engaged in lately at work. Good riddance to the games and to her. It wasn't until he was back at the elevator that it hit him, though. The woman had gotten the best of him. Gotten the last word. No one had done that to Marshall Wilder. With the possible exception of Jenifer, but she'd had lawyers at her back while his own had kept his hands tied.

No, he couldn't let this victory of hers stand. He'd have to strike back. He was captain of the ship. Without his authority, they would all go under. Authority meant discipline. No one left the presence of Marshall Wilder without permission. Nor were they allowed to quit. Rifling through the nightstand drawer he pulled out the phone book. Yellow and antiquated.

There was a page and a half devoted to Hunters. He found no Meridian, but there were two with the first initial M. One was in Rosewood, thirty miles south. The other was on Thirty-Fifth Street, downtown. Bingo.

Tearing out the page, he smiled to himself. Miss Hunter was in for a little surprise tonight. He was going to have the last word, and make her retract that resignation.

And then he was going to fire her.

* * * * *

Merrie wanted to tear the clothing from her body. She hated the dress almost as much as she hated the man who'd made her wear it for him. Had she said man? Unspeakable, disgusting, lying worm was far more to the point. He'd tricked her, torn out her heart. Violated her. She would never forgive him. Never look him in the eye. Never work for him. Never even give him the benefit of a resignation letter.

Peeling off the humiliating clothing—god, how he'd played her for a fool—she threw herself into the shower. Full blast. She needed the water to cleanse herself. She felt so used, so foolish. Fighting back the tears, she concentrated on the scrubbing. Never again would she go to that website or that hotel. Never again would she dream of a strong man. Or any man for that matter.

The doorbell must have been ringing for a long time. She turned off the water and reached for a towel. It was probably Kennedy, who had infallible radar for this sort of thing. Wrapping the large, thirsty bath towel around her torso, she dripped her way to the door. Company was the last thing she wanted, but she knew from experience the woman would keep this up until she answered.

In most ways, Kennedy was like the annoying little sister Merrie had never wanted. The sister who drives you crazy most of the time, but who you find after a while you can't live without. Merrie almost forgot to check the peephole she was so sure who was there. Her heart seized in her chest when she saw it was him. Impossible. There was no way the man could have this much gall. She pushed her eye closer, just to see if she was hallucinating.

It was Wilder, all right. Looking uncharacteristically disheveled. And he was soaking wet, too. Had it started raining outside?

"Miss Hunter, are you there? I can hear you breathing."

Merrie jumped back from the door like it was electrified. Did the man have ESP on top of everything else?

"You shouldn't be here," she said, trying to sound as imposing as possible. "If you don't leave at once, I'll call the police."

Merrie looked back through the peephole to see what he would do. He had his hands in his pockets. He was shivering, looking pathetic. He didn't even have a raincoat on.

"You're not getting rid of me that easily." He paused to sneeze. "If I have to, I'll buy the damned building."

Merrie bit her lip to fight back a chuckle. She really did not need to be laughing at a time like this. Nor did she need to be feeling sorry for the man. Not after what he'd done to her.

"Go buy yourself a towel instead. I already quit. What more do you want from me?"

He sneezed again. "Five minutes of your time. I think you owe me that much at least."

Her pity turned to fury. Fingers flying over the chain and double locks, she flung open the door to confront him directly. "I owe *you*?" She spat the words back at him so he could hear how preposterous they were. "I'm not the one who lied about his identity and totally humiliated and disgraced an unsuspecting woman, am I?"

Marshall scowled, obviously not used to being caught dead to rights. "I did what I did for your own good, to protect you. Suppose I'd been some rapist or serial killer?"

"I'd have preferred it. At least those kinds of criminals just commit one single crime and leave—but you, you planned to torture me my whole life with this, didn't you?"

He released a low growl. "Blast it, woman, stop being so childish, before I take you over my knee!"

That was all Meridian needed to hear. Oblivious of her near nudity, she launched herself at him, fists flying. "I'll give you childish!" she declared.

Wilder seized both her wrists, effortlessly. "What in blazes has gotten into you?" he demanded. "Calm down at once."

Merrie kneed him in the groin. "How's that for calm?"

Marshall grimaced, releasing her. "Dammit," he groaned, bracing himself against the doorframe. "Are you trying to cripple me?"

She slashed at his face with her nails. "Yes. Now get out of here! Who said you could be in my doorway, anyway?"

Wilder issued a mild epithet. This gave Merrie just enough time to grab the ceramic kitten off the table in the foyer and bonk him on the head with it.

The man bent forward under the impact, making a strange noise.

Oh, god, what had she just done?

"Mr. Wilder? Are you all right?"

"Of course…I'm not all right," he managed to sputter in broken syllables. "I've just been kneed in groin…and assaulted by…whatever in hell that was."

"It's a replica of Simon the Cat. From the comic strip, and I've got another one here I'll use if you—"

Wilder grabbed her wrist before she could employ her next weapon of choice. He must have been a little dazed, because he cursed her out, calling her Jenifer.

"I'm Meridian," she squirmed, forgetting for the moment that her only garment was the towel.

"You might as well be," he said, "the way you're trying to fuck with my head—inside and out."

"I'm not trying to be anyone or do anything," she protested, but it was too late. He had her by the upper arms and he was drawing her close. The kiss was hot and demanding, not at all that of a wounded man. She had about as much chance of resisting as a lamb did a hungry lion.

"Mr. Wilder…" She tried to separate her lips, but he had them, along with the rest of her. Her poor little body was defenseless, the terrycloth offering no protection from his hard muscles. She felt the wetness between her legs, the tight little tingling in her engorged nipples.

"You've no idea," he breathed directly into her mouth. "How long I've waited. What I've been through."

"No, I don't," she squirmed. "And you can't hold me responsible."

"Some women," he said, his sentences breaking into short stabbing phrases, "are born to be owned. To be branded. Taken. Named by a Master."

"I'm not one of them," she cried, though she was not at all certain anymore.

Whoever he thought she was, Jenifer, Meridian, ownmenow, and for that matter, whoever he was, Wilder, Master Nightshade or just some crazy, sopping wet man who'd shown up at her door out of the blue, there was no denying what was happening between them.

The dance. The fencing. The finding of places, ancient and acutely sexual that the two of them had been talking about online so intently for the last few days.

"Sir…" Her heart was racing.

"That's right," he encouraged, sounding almost intoxicated. "I'm your superior. We can't deny that…not now, not tonight…tomorrow, maybe, but not now."

Wilder wanted between her lips and got it. His tongue went deep, exploring, marking, branding. She had no choice, no wish, even, but to open. A moan escaped her throat, muffled by his mouth as he undid the towel and yanked it away. Her suddenly nude body molded instantly to his clothed one. The wetness of his shirt and khakis, clinging to undeniable muscle underneath, only adding to her feelings of wicked, sensuous helplessness.

"You're so beautiful, Meridian. No man would ever let you stay free, do you know that?"

They were not equal and he was letting her know it. She was a female—he'd wanted her naked and so she was. He wanted her aroused, kissed to submission, and he was getting that, too. Testing him now, in a futile show of resistance, she tried to push at his chest and turn her face away.

"This can't go any further. It's not good for either of us."

"Hands down," he commanded. "Stand still."

The edict was enforced with his hand at the back of her neck, fingers gripping and pulling back the center section of her long, shimmering copper hair. It was another kiss he wanted, a contact of such power and mastery as to make the other look like child's play.

"Ohh..." she moaned. "Oh, god."

Merrie's arms fell. She could feel her spine giving way. The man read her perfectly, swooping in to seize her up. The next thing she knew, she was in his arms, looking up at his determined face, lit by an otherworldly glow. Did she dare ask what all of this meant to him? His cock was like steel under the clinging, soggy pants. There was no mistaking what he'd do to her with it, how he'd use her. Already, she could feel her pussy clenching in anticipation. Was it too late to stop this?

In the back of her mind, came a last, small voice of sanity. It was her right to resist and maybe her obligation. Before something happened that they would both regret in the morning.

"Mr. Wilder...Marshall," she said as softly as possible, hating to break the spell as he laid her in the middle of her own bed. "It doesn't have to be this way."

"Yes," he assured her. "It does." His hand was between her legs, his fingers easily parting her sex lips. She'd been wet from the moment he came to the door, praying he wouldn't smell it on her, and now he'd have the evidence for himself. It would be all he needed to complete his conquest.

"Oh, sir," she moaned, as he stroked her vulnerable little clit, instantly swollen from the commanding touch of her would-be lover. "Please don't."

But Meridian didn't want him to stop. Ever. If he did, she was sure she would die. So much need in her, so much pent-up tension. Her body was already writhing, already inviting, already welcoming.

"Sir," she cried again, the title taking on a whole new meaning as he played her expertly, claiming in real life the role he'd assumed as online Master of her flesh. "What are you doing to me?"

"Giving you what you need. What you've been crying out for all along."

He had her body purring. Revving. She felt like she was at the auto shop, just standing by, the mechanic working on her engine, a mechanism she hardly understood, and which was totally under his power. With the lightest of manipulations, he flicked her nipples. "See how big they become?"

"They've never looked like that," she exclaimed. "Never so tight."

Next he grazed her belly, working his way downward to press the inner walls of her pussy with a single fingertip. "It's time for me to show you what your body can do in the right hands."

"Oh, god, I thought of this online," she confessed. "I thought of you."

"So did I. But there's no future in this," he lamented. "This is fleeting…for the moment."

"Then we should stop."

"No," he shook his head, his face an odd mix of pleasure and torture. "We have to go on. To cure ourselves. Don't you see? Men and women can't sustain this energy? It kills…relationships, hope?"

She didn't see, though, she only felt as again and again, he worked his way up and down, his fingers dabbing her lips, caressing her earlobes, teasing her knees—a hundred different places—from the hollow of her neck, to the tip of her nose and the bottoms of her feet, making it all sexual, every little inch of her flesh.

"Sir, I'm...falling."

"It's all right, just let go."

Groans escaped her throat, deep but very female. There was no time to think, no time to hold back. It was too much to look into those eyes, and thank god he wasn't asking her to. She feared associating these new feelings with those stormy blue depths. If she should make that link...between this and him, she feared she would really become his, dependent in a way no woman, least of all an independent career woman on her way up the ladder could afford.

"Never been...like this," she stammered. Merrie felt the spasms in her very bones and nerves before they actually came to fruition. Wherever the hell he'd built this orgasm up from, whatever new kind it was, it was not going to come at her in any way she could control.

"Let it go," he repeated, the authority of his voice doing the trick.

It was like a full-body climax, designed to open her, to make her lift her pelvis and arch her back and offer her mouth, all without any prospect of contact with his cock. Like coming and being teased at the same time.

"Sir," she moaned. "Tell me...tell me you want me."

"Oh, god, yes, more than you can know."

She looked up at him and saw that his shirt was off, revealing his mouth-watering chest. His hair was much darker looking wet, and his chest glistened a little from the rain.

"No," he slapped her hand away as she tried to touch him.

"It's not fair," she whined.

"It's not supposed to be," he reminded.

"Yes, sir," Merrie humbled herself. He was right. This was all part of the game. She was the slave and he was her Master Nightshade, at least to the extent he'd claimed her on that foolish site in the first place.

A woman's body was something to be played for him, it was clear, and his smooth, strong hands seemed born for the task. But why her in particular, lying naked like this, made a fool of, fucked with the man's hand for his personal sport, in her own bed after he'd humiliated her online and made her come to one of the fanciest hotels in the city dressed like a whore? Surely he had lots of bimbos to choose from.

Was she the only one who danced at his touch, who'd been privileged to come alive at the feel of his fingers marking her hips or her cheeks or breasts?

The anger welled inside her and with it a sudden determination to resist. Who in hell did this man think he was? He wouldn't have her this way. She wouldn't allow it.

"I don't like this anymore," Merrie tried to sit up, only to have him grasp her nipple, vise-like, between his thumb and forefinger. It was a gritty, merciless contact that made a shudder run up and down her spine. The downward pressure left her no option but to abandon her rebellion and lie back. She ground her teeth in futility.

"You're hurting me," she whimpered, though really it was an act of mild disciplinary control and not one of sadism. "You're a…horrible man."

"Tell me to leave, then."

"I will…when I'm good and ready," she said quite irrationally.

Wilder's response to her tacit invitation to go on was swift and severe. Moving his hands just so, lowering his mouth possessively to her breast, he demolished her in another orgasm, this time a suckling one that made her press against him with every part of herself, needing the contact for her very existence. The scream from the back of her throat was entirely silent. It was like the man had laid explosive charges throughout her body and now he was setting them off.

"Oh, god that feels good." Wilder's fingers and tongue and teeth continued to work in devastating harmony as he hovered above her. Merrie's body was a chasm, emptied and now refilled with the reverberations and echoes of desperate need. Red hair tossing, green eyes burning, pink nipples throbbing. More than anything, she was a sacrifice, laid on a river of silk, awaiting the will of her man. She wanted to be groped, to be fucked, but it wasn't about her. Meridian was giving what he wanted, her complete and utter self-offering, with him detached, controlling, observing her responses, his cock as yet untried. All of this only made her feel more aroused…more like…a slave.

"Hold me," she reached for him and he gathered both of her wrists in one hand. His face spoke of iron control and denial. The sudden restraint as he pinned them above her head sent her into a whole new round of convulsions. She was coming against her will, or at least not as a result of it. This was his doing and she was only a vessel, a plaything for his amusement.

She thrashed her head, trying to focus on something, needing something to anchor her womanly instincts. "Marshall?"

Had she said that out loud? She wanted to eat him up with the sound of his name, devour his cock and lick his balls, press her lips to his stomach, nuzzle his hair, fall prostrate before him, and a million more things besides.

Her body pressed upwards, trying to orient itself in the void, seeking to map itself against his skin, his flesh, his world. But there were miles between them. A gulf of pleasure…and of agony, sweet building agony, such that however much she felt, there would always be more. More she'd have to have, more she couldn't do without. Was this slavery? To want to be fucked more than anything in the world and also to be held in the process like no one had ever held her before? At once to be delivered, denied, delayed and thwarted, however the Master wanted it?

Wilder took two, three more orgasms from her this way, or maybe a hundred. Then again, it might have been only the one long one. It was like standing inside a hurricane, or a jungle shower that washes over you, pleasuring every pore of your skin, taking from you all resistance, the water sluicing into every crevice, the beat of the falling rain a drum of bliss, the whipping winds like a lover's searing passion.

He only stopped when there was nothing left of her, only melted sweat. Sweet, elusive juices born of other juices, a wispy essence of woman, but at the same time an all too flesh and blood body, the dream of any man, primed and ready. No ability, no mind to resist.

Merrie concentrated on her breathing, still not able to look at him. Somewhere above her he floated and she tried to stay objective, to hold onto some facet of her reason, herself. He was taking off the rest of his clothes. Letting her see, making her see. Slowly, deliberately and casually he opened his pants, the motions advertising the capabilities of his lean and muscular chest, the envy of any weekend warrior, any gym hanger-on. He wasn't overly developed, but perfectly so, like he'd distilled his body to what was pure male, that combination of muscle and smooth flesh meant to bring the female of the species to her knees.

Merrie wasn't sure who else had seen this chest, the hard biceps, raised pectorals and six-pack abdomen, but she couldn't imagine that any woman at all, even this elusive Jenifer, could possibly have remained immune to its power and spell once exposed. His body, she decided, was no less dangerous than his eyes. Even now it was drawing her in, promising things. Demanding things.

Her breath caught in her throat as he pulled off the khakis leaving only his underwear. So it was real then. Meridian Hunter was going to be had by her boss, by the man who—online—had called himself her Master. Her sexual owner. This would be a real good time to fight, but for some reason her muscles wouldn't move. In part, she told herself, this was because she knew he was stronger, and that she could never stop him from putting his cock inside her, if that's what he wanted.

It was not only Marshall she was dealing with, it was Master Nightshade, the ruthless cybernetic Master who had made her pinch her own nipples and smack her own ass until it turned hot and red. Once she'd had to do the dishes naked with clothespins on her labia and another time she'd had to fuck herself with a cucumber, orgasming every five minutes for half an hour.

I must please him, she thought, feeling like the most wicked, wanton whore in the history of the world. *I must please this man's cock. He is my Master. If I disobey, if I am not good enough, he will punish me, beat me, humiliate me, or, as he threatened to do online, share me with his friends.*

Merrie gasped as he pulled the boxers down over his blood-engorged shaft. It was already so thick and hard, a living, vibrant thing. The sight of it mesmerized her. So smooth and pretty and pulsing like a sculpture to admire and yet there was no denying what it would do to her. Soon, very soon, it would be deep inside her, where it would manipulate and control and possess her.

She glared hungrily at the tip of it, a tiny glistening drop of pre-come poised, as if waiting for her thirsty tongue. She wanted to taste it, to wrap her senses around it, around him.

Wilder's balls were hanging full and heavy beneath his cock. There was sperm in those sacs, white-hot liquid, which he would shoot deep inside her. In her pussy if he chose, or, if he preferred, her mouth. Even her ass, if that was what he wanted. She would take it, wherever and however, and she would orgasm with him if that was his command. How many times had he made her do that at her own keyboard—after forcing her to beg and beg, humiliating herself with her typed pleas?

And what orgasms they'd been, her leg tucked underneath her, rocking and moaning and crying, her pussy clenching and unclenching like he was with her, inside her, like she had the power to suck him all the way through the Internet to fill her.

"Tell me what you need, Meridian."

He was waiting to possess her, making her say the words first. She writhed, pinned by his glare, by his raw dominance. She was so helpless and so at home in that helplessness. The man was naked before her, about to do something to her unlike what any other man had ever done and there was no stopping it. No anticipating, either. With her eyes, she begged for mercy, making the mistake of looking wholly into his gaze.

He was a Greek statue, looming, the eyes of a celestial god coming towards her, coming for her, a look of complete and total desire and possession upon his face. She felt more possessed in that glance than she had in the full embrace of all her previous partners combined.

"I need...you, Master."

He seized her pussy with his whole hand, owning it. "Not good enough. Not specific enough."

"I need to be fucked," she said quickly.

Turning her slightly, he smacked her ass. Hard.

"I need to be fucked, *Master,*" she corrected herself.

"Yes," he agreed, "you do."

Merrie bit her lip. How would she ever survive his touch, she despaired, let alone full penetration? She ached from the warmth of his approaching body. He was crawling upon her like a tiger. His eyes never leaving hers, riveted and denying her any chance to look away. He had her, fixed and locked. She was going to be his. Any second now, at his total bidding. But where would he start, and how, using that magnificent body of his, would he complete her conquest?

She could smell him, the musk of his cologne mixed with elemental manhood, the thrumming of his heartbeat in the air, the slight waft of perspiration beaded on his forehead. Her body shivered, she sucked in her breath, retreating against the mattress, and yet all the femaleness of her still reached for him, the oversensitive nipples, conveying far too much, easy knobs to twist at her insides, and her vulva, each little nerve ending in her soft puckered lips beckoning, begging.

"What are you?" he said now, the words spoken directly into her ear.

"Your slave," she hissed without hesitation. "Your slave, Master."

Everything became slow motion as he mounted, taking his position as though he'd been born for this, and her, too. She spasmed at the touch of him, his lips grazing her neck at the exact moment the head of his thick, throbbing cock poised itself between her legs. She wanted to thrust up at him, but she had no power. She must wait upon him, wait upon his will. He was teasing her, the elapsed seconds like centuries.

His teeth dug into her neck, clamping and she cried out, though there was little sound, little air in her lungs. Whimpers escaped her throat and moans of "oh, god," as his cock descended, at last, at long last. Inch by inch, releasing from her body the most intimate of female sounds, baring the most intimate of female needs.

She was a woman, pure and clean, being fucked by a man. Gorgeous, elemental and full of strength. Complicated too—the man, and the relationship—but still the easiest thing in the world, to take him to the hilt...so wet so ready.

"Omigod...ohmy..." Merrie wrapped her legs around him, clenching her ankles together.

A low grunt from his gut as he pulled out, nearly to the brink, and slammed home again. She dug into his back with her nails but the pain, however much he was feeling, only seemed to encourage him. He was steering this ship, making it happen. Making her happen.

They fucked like animals. Pure and simple passion, gnawing teeth, mingled sweat. She creamed and moaned, and came, actively encouraging him as he spanked her ass and pinched her nipples, pushing her into whatever position he wanted. Everything was coming out of her, completely unglued, and him like a roaring beast, untamed, but completely under control at the same time. This man, this Master could handle anything. Handle her, her passion, and his to boot.

She clutched at him and screamed out her surrender at the top of her lungs, and it was as if she had never had an orgasm before. Like he was her first lover, taking her virginity all over again. Every part of her felt supremely sexual and alive and used and lusted after and loved. Lip to lip, murmuring and moaning, hands groping and claiming. Belly to belly, breast to breast—hers full and round against his hard chest—pelvis locked to pelvis, the head of his cock buried deep in her canal, pushing against her womb, a shuddering between bodies that spoke, worked through things, and raised questions. So many damned questions.

His own orgasm provided the only answer she needed, though. It was a thundering cascade, washing away what remained of her reason. His cock thick and hard, exploding and filling and owning. On and on, his muscles tensed, but pulsing with the pain, as his life, his flesh and blood poured into her. Until there was nothing left to separate them, nothing to break this union.

For a long time she simply continued glowing, the orange ember of a spent flame. Their limbs still intertwined, they accepted, for the moment, the reality, the limitations of their physical bodies.

He mumbled something into her left breast, while he took the other in his hand. Merrie orgasmed again from the touch and from the intimate form of possessiveness it represented. Tears, clean and fresh came down her cheeks. She didn't know why she was crying, except that she was getting something she'd always dreamed of, never having known until now exactly what it was.

If only it weren't with the wrong man. The wrong time. The wrong reality. For a few moments, she contemplated pushing him off of her, but he was breathing so peacefully. He needed his rest, a man like this. Probably never slept right half the time, and who knew his diet. Idly, she thought of cooking for him. Lord, but her mind was going in foolish directions. The day she had any sympathy for a tyrant like this was the day…well, it was a far off, impossible day, that's all she would say about it.

Sighing deeply, she tuned back into his heartbeat. She had the right to enjoy that, just for a second. And if she closed her eyes and happened to fall asleep, well she had that right as well. After all he'd put her through, it was the least he could do for her as far as she was concerned.

* * * * *

Marshall Wilder awoke with his hand cupped on the moist vagina of Meridian Hunter. He was lying with his head on her chest, on top of her full breasts. The woman was asleep, obviously post-coitus. With a start he sat up. By god, what had he done?

Okay, it was clear what he'd done. The question was why? He'd come here, in the rain, to see her after she'd run out of the hotel. To talk her out of resigning so he could fire her—as if that made any sense. But then he'd seen her at the door, wearing nothing but a towel, so vulnerable and angry and so very completely female, and all thoughts of business disappeared from his mind. All of a sudden he'd wanted her, more than he had any woman in his life.

Wanted her in his bed, and on her knees, and every other way a woman could submit to a man. She had had no idea of her effect on him, clearly. He grimaced, looking at her sex-stained body. Obviously by now she had some clue. Wilder slipped off the bed, allowing himself one final look at the copper-haired sprite. Her hair was in wild tangles about her face, her lips were pouting softly in her sleep and her palms were upturned. Her magnificent sculpted breasts rose and fell in time to her breathing. The nipples were tiny pink buds set in small, pretty areolas.

He loved her belly best of all, with its slight indentation, a gentle white valley, bespeaking health and a total, complete sexiness that led the eyes so naturally to her delta. The sight of it made him shiver. Had he really been inside this creature? Filled her with his cock, his sperm?

Yes, the evidence was there, the dried residue that had oozed from between her sex lips onto her fiery thatch. God, he wanted her once more, all over again, in bondage this time, her wrists and ankles tied spread-eagled. The look on her face as she anticipated her ravishing would be exquisite.

Almost unconsciously, he began to stroke himself. Little Miss ownmenow had indeed been owned, at least for an interval by Master Nightshade. It had seemed so cut and dried online. Just going through the motions of being the eager, predatory Dominant, luring her into his web. But now he had to wonder. Had it been so easy and natural for him for a reason? Was there some deeper connection between him and this woman?

Wilder's shaft was like iron. Blood pulsed along the veins of it. He gripped it tightly, holding on for dear life, the undersides of his fingers squeezing just how he liked best. He wished he had a better memory of being inside her pussy. It had all been kind of foggy at the time. His head in a daze. Damn it, had he called her Jenifer? That was bad form, to be sure, not to mention the reliving of a personal nightmare on his end.

What about this experience last night—this new woman had brought that out? Once again, Miss Hunter had managed to break through carefully laid defenses that had been put there for the good of himself and everyone else.

Pushing his hand all the way to the base of his cock, he focused on the sleeping form of the angelic Meridian. He needed to banish Jenifer's memory. And then, after that, this woman's too. It was well past time to be ruled by his cock in that regard. There was no pretending anymore that getting his rocks off had anything to do with love. Or that love itself even existed except as a silly, overblown form of lust, a house of cards that comes crashing down, inevitably, once the sex cools off.

Should he feel guilty masturbating over his employee like this? No more so than he should for screwing her brains out as he'd done earlier. Okay, time to get this over with, he thought. Licking his lips, he worked himself up to full speed. Putting out his left hand he prepared to catch the white-hot issue. Eyes clenched shut, he concentrated on purging. Purifying himself of every unwanted female image.

Unfortunately, Meridian remained in his mind's eye. Irrepressible, as it were. She was nude, her hair wild and free, on her hands and knees, crawling to him, to take his dick in her mouth. She wouldn't take no for an answer.

"Use me, Master," she whispered in his imagination. "Use my mouth."

Wilder held back the grunt as he came. It was deep and satisfying, the sperm covering his palm. It took several more strokes to work it all out and bring himself down from the self-induced high. As quickly as possible afterwards, being in his right mind again, he found his clothes, dressed and left Miss Hunter's apartment.

Out of all of it, the entire sordid mess, the only consolation he had was that he would never have to see her again as long as he lived. Because if she ever did try and show up at his building again, he would have security remove her. In a heartbeat.

Chapter Four

Oscar, the building's faithful old security guard, was standing at the front door when Meridian arrived the next morning for work. He looked distressed, as unhappy as she'd ever seen the man.

"Miss Hunter, I'm sorry, but I have orders not to let you in."

Merrie's face went crimson. That bastard Wilder wasn't even going to let her collect her personal effects. Unbelievable. Of course this was the same man who'd pretended to be someone else online, claiming it was all an excuse to keep her from going around picking up men off the Internet, only to go ahead and fuck her for real afterwards. And what a fuck it was. A fantastic, mind-blowing, heart-wrenching one-night stand, without so much as a one-line note of explanation afterwards. If she were a man, she would take this Marshall Wilder to the nearest back alley and beat the living tar out of him.

"Oscar, I'm here for my things. I've resigned," she pleaded her case. "Just let me upstairs, I'll be in and out in less than five minutes."

The beefy Hispanic man's face contorted. "Miss Hunter, I'd do anything for you, you know I would…but it's my job on the line, and you know Rosa is out of work now, and…"

Merrie sighed. It wasn't fair of her to put Oscar in this position. Yes, she'd been the one to help him keep this job three years ago when he had a drinking problem, but now there was a new boss and he had to toe the line as much as anyone else.

"It's all right, Oscar. I'm sorry I even suggested it. I'll just sneak around the side door. Kennedy will let me in."

"I'm sorry, ma'am, but we can't allow that," pronounced a gruff, unfamiliar voice. "Mr. Wilder's orders."

The man wore a red jacket, a blazer with a gold embroidered Wilder Industries logo on the jacket pocket. He was one of Marshall's new corporate security men—goons—as far as she was concerned.

"Mr. Wilder can go to the devil," she defied.

A second red blazer showed up, equally broad-shouldered with a yellow crew cut in place of the other man's black one. "Is there a problem here?"

She noted the silver pin on his lapel. He must be in charge. "Yes, you and your boss are the problem."

"Ma'am, we need to escort you back to your car. This is private property and you're trespassing."

Wilder was low, all right, but she hadn't known just how low until this minute. "I'll go on my own," she kept her dignity. "And I'll thank you to tell the great Mr. Wilder I would as soon step on a pile of scorpions than set foot on his precious private property ever again."

The two guards frowned, first at her, then at each other. Walkie-talkies squawking in their pockets, they followed her out to her convertible. Her hands trembled as she started the engine, though she managed nonetheless to take off with a proper flourish, peeling rubber.

For a half hour or so she drove around the city aimlessly. Kennedy was trying to call her on her cell phone, but she wasn't in the mood to talk. She considered just driving up to the mountains or maybe over to the coast to see how her dad was doing. In the end, without even realizing where she'd been going, she found herself back at work, right across the street from the building that should have been hers to run.

Wilder's Porsche was parked right in front, a painful reminder of his continued existence on the planet, not to mention his high and mighty position, untouchable and aloof. Of course, he'd probably forgotten all about her by now and what he'd done to her. Ooh, how she hated the man. Maybe some vigilante justice was in order. In the back of her mind she knew this wasn't very smart, but she was a woman on a mission, albeit a kooky one. Leaving her car safely out of sight, she snuck across the street. It was midmorning by now and no one was in the parking lot.

In movies and on TV she'd seen people mess with ignition wires or pour sugar into gas tanks, but she didn't know how to open his hood and she seriously doubted the one packet of sugar in her purse would make all that much difference in his driving performance. If she was really devious, she could foul up his brakes, cut the line thingies or something. That would make a pretty picture. Him sailing around some curve in a box canyon, thinking he has the world by the tail, only to find as he presses that nice safe pedal to the floor that he is screwed, screwed, screwed.

Bye, bye, Mr. Billionaire Liar. Over the edge of the cliff you go.

But she didn't really have it in her heart to kill anyone. Not even the ants she sometimes found in her kitchen. Besides, she knew nothing about cars. Except tires. She knew that tires held air and without the air, they go flat and the driver doesn't go anywhere. Grinning wickedly, she formulated her plan.

She would deflate Marshall Wilder's tires. Leave him high and dry.

But what could she use? A screwdriver would have been nice. Or a knife. Unfortunately, she had only her keys. Would they be sharp enough? Maybe she could let the air out of the valve stem. Kneeling was a little hard in her skirt so she squatted. The cap unscrewed easily enough, though she couldn't figure out how to push in the little release thingy for the air. As a last resort she tried to use her apartment key.

It was in this very position, poking away in utter futility that he found her. "Would you like to use my Swiss Army knife? You'd get a lot further."

Merrie froze at the sound of Wilder's voice. *Fuck. Fuck. Double fuck.*

The man loomed above her, six feet of smug, towering manhood. As quickly and gracefully as possible she stood to confront him. "You had no right to keep me out of my office. All I wanted was to collect my things."

"I'll have them delivered to your residence," he said without emotion, his blue eyes nicely offset today by a dark blue shirt, gray print tie and black suit.

She looked for some chink in that armor of his, some way to get at him, but found none. "That's very kind of you. I'm sure you'll send me the bill for it as well," she said curtly.

"I'll deduct it," he ignored her sarcasm, "from your severance."

"I hate you," she informed him.

His lips thinned almost imperceptibly. "Go home, Meridian. It's over."

He'd never used her first name before. The sound of it made her weak in the knees, though under the circumstances it was just one more slap in the face. "No," she told him coldly. "Not yet."

The key was still in her hand, clenched so tightly it was pinching her skin. Reaching out to run the sharp metal across the silver-flecked paint of the Porsche's door was sheer instinct, an act of anger born deep within. The high-pitched sound of metal scraping was jarring, but eminently satisfying at the same time.

"There," she examined the deep, jagged gouge in the door. "Now it's over."

Marshall had her wrist, preventing her from making her intended theatrical exit. His eyes meant business and she was more than a little uncertain of his intent.

"Let go of me, Wilder. I'm not kidding."

"You and I need to take a little ride," he said, his voice as calm as she'd ever heard it.

"Over your dead body," she scoffed. "And trust me, I have thought of enough ways to make that little fantasy of mine come true."

And indeed she had in the time since she'd woken in the wee hours this morning to find herself naked, alone and rejected. The smell of the man, his sperm even, on her body, but no trace of his living presence. She tried crying, even throwing things—she did this until she ran out of ceramic cartoon animals—but nothing had eased the pain, the confusion, the empty, gnawing place inside her.

No, it wasn't his tires she wanted to cut out at all, but his heart. The problem was he didn't have one.

"I think we can do without the histrionics, don't you?" he queried.

Merrie spat a phrase back at him, none too polite. It was one she seldom used, even under the direst of circumstances.

"I am not fond of women using off-color language," he informed her.

He really was unbelievable. Totally, freaking, out-to-lunch.

"What do you expect?" She shot back, with uncharacteristic cattiness. "I'm Jenifer. The little bitch. Remember? Or do you only confuse us when you're between my legs?"

Marshall's eyes lit. His lips tightened as if he was going to say something nasty. For a split second, she thought she was going to have him dead to rights, goading him into actually showing human emotion. A moment later, however, he returned to his Spock-like control.

"Let's just get in the car," he ushered her towards the scarred door. "We are accomplishing nothing at this rate."

His hand on her back, gently but firmly guiding her, telegraphed volumes. It was a commanding gesture, but also one that warmed her at once through the blouse. As if somehow her skin had remembered the man's touch and was responding.

"You don't own me," she protested, even as her treacherous body acted as if he did, allowing him to seat her in the obnoxiously expensive car without the slightest bit of resistance. "I'm a free woman."

"Really?" He sat down heavily in the driver's seat. "Seems to me you haven't enough control to claim self-ownership."

"What the hell is that supposed to mean?" she demanded.

"Your behavior," he turned the key in the ignition, "is that of a spoiled child. Not a free, adult woman."

"Me?" She laughed at the absurdity. "I'm not the one who goes around acting like a seventeen year-old boy, lying to innocent women just to get his rocks off. Oh, wait, that's giving you too much credit. Let's change that to a manipulative evil monkey boy, shall we?"

Wilder downshifted, stone-faced. "It was you who put yourself up, essentially for sale on Xchange.com," he declared. "Thanks to me you were spared the humiliation you deserved. In response to my gesture, instead of thanking me, you have pouted, abandoned your post, letting down your fellow workers, and now you have sunk to the level of petty vandalism."

Merrie had never wanted to scratch out a man's eyes so much. And if they weren't already on the expressway where the slightest wobbling of the wheel would ensure both of their deaths, she would already be on him. What she needed to do was to keep things calm so he'd let her out of this car as quickly as possible.

"Where are you taking me?" She folded her arms. "And why?"

"I am taking you to be punished," said her former boss, as though it were the most natural thing in the world.

"Excuse me?"

"Your behavior in scratching my car was that of a miscreant child, so I'm going to treat you like one."

Merrie's heart thundered in her chest. "I don't know what you're talking about, Wilder, but if you don't let me out now, I'm going to scream for the next police car I see."

"I think you know exactly what I mean...and I think you've been asking for it all along. Haven't you, little Miss ownmenow?"

Merrie's pussy flooded, a reflex that greatly weakened her pretenses of hating the man's plans. "Anything you do to me will be against my will," she vowed. "You'll go to jail."

Wilder laughed. It was tight and dry and it was the first time she'd ever heard such a sound coming from the man's mouth. "Do you think you fool me for a second, young lady? I can smell your sex from here. You want this so bad you can taste it."

Merrie blushed hotly, clamping her thighs together. "You're a pig," she cried. "A total pig."

"Indeed," he said, somewhat ominously for her tastes. "And that is exactly how you want me to be, isn't it?"

"I don't know what you're talking about." She tried to sound aloof and contemptuous though in her belly she was pulsing with a dread desire.

"What I'm talking about," he accelerated into the third lane to pass a barreling semi, "is that you clearly have not learned your lesson. Or else you'd be thanking me profusely and abjectly. So that means I need to make the point a little more obvious."

"What point is that? As if I cared."

"That BDSM is not for nice girls like you."

"I'm a woman, not a girl."

"See? That's my point. A true slave would let me call her a girl and like it."

"I'm sure you find nice little bimbos like that every day," she spat. "But what has this to do with me?"

"Everything, my dear. Everything. I'm about to cure you, once and for all, of your fixation with all things leather."

"Is that right, Dr. Freud? And how exactly do you intend to do that?"

"By giving you a dose of what you think you want, Meridian. Slavery and all that comes with it."

Merrie's stomach did a flip and slide. A flock of butterflies soared to the height of ecstasy, only to sink into unspeakable oblivion. "W-What are you talking about, Wilder?"

"We are going to my cabin in the mountains," he said. "For the next three days, you will live with me…as my slave. During that time, I will protect you and keep you safe—allowing no permanent mental or physical damage to come to you—but you can be assured that by the end you will never want to go near an alternative lifestyle website, or even a movie, poster or book as long as you live."

Merrie's heart was in her throat. "You don't scare me," she lied. "Not even a little."

"I'm not trying to scare you," he said. "Or threaten you. I'm just telling you the facts."

"The only facts I know are that you are crazy and you are going to jail for kidnapping, as soon as I can manage it."

"That may be," he acknowledged. "But for now…slave girl…you are mine."

"D-Don't," she protested as his hand found her thigh. She tried to pry it loose, but the man's fingers only gripped her more tightly.

"A slave girl has no rights, Meridian. Not even to her own body. That is your first lesson." His hand moved under the hem of the pleated skirt. She was wearing no stockings today, which meant there was nothing to separate her bare skin from his kneading fingers. "Open your legs, slave girl."

She shook her head, more out of desperation than real resolve. Wilder was ready for this. "Disobedience means punishment, Meridian. That is your second lesson. Are you ready to accept the consequences for your actions…on your bare ass?"

Merrie separated her thighs.

"Wider," he commanded.

She gave a little moan as she spread her legs. She was sopping wet, and throbbing with need.

"Recline your seat, grasp the headrest supports with both hands," he ordered. "And do not remove them without further instructions."

Merrie lowered the seat and felt behind her. The supports to the headrest were thin metal rods. They felt cool against her damp palms.

"I didn't intend it to come to this," he glanced at his self-imprisoned passenger. "But you've left me no choice."

"Mr. Wilder…Marshall," she croaked. "Whatever you're going to do…please…don't."

"It's too late for that," he shook his head. "From here on in, you will call me 'Master'. Is that clear?"

"Y-Yes," she heard her lips pronounce, as though they belonged to someone else. "Master."

Wilder flipped up her skirt, revealing the pink, baby doll panties she'd chosen at random in her early a.m. haze.

"Charming," he remarked, "and very indicative of your innate femininity. As a slave, of course, your choice of clothing—inner or outer—is determined by your Master. You receive everything at his whim, every scrap of material, even the food you are allowed. To a true slave, this is the ultimate turn-on. To be controlled, to have no choice but to be pleasing to the one who holds absolute power over her. I've never met such a woman myself. Except in stories. Ridiculous fiction that serves no purpose but to deceive men and women equally. But you wanted to play the game, and so we will."

His fingers slipped under the waistband of the drenched panties. "For three days, Meridian, we will live this fantasy, you and I. Ever heard the old story about the boy and the box of cigars? He sneaks a cigar from his father. The father catches him smoking it and decides to cure him of the desire by making him smoke the whole box. Overexposure, Meridian, that's what we are aiming for."

Her pussy clenched at his teasing fingers. "Oh," she moaned. "Oh, Master."

"Another rule, Meridian. Orgasms are a privilege. Earned. Coming without permission results in more punishment."

"Yes," she gasped. "Master."

"You may writhe against my fingers."

Desperately, she sought the contact, trying to make enough pressure to ease the ache, the hollow, sweet yearning, raised so quickly to fever pitch.

"Slave girls are allowed no pride. You'll learn that, too."

Meridian grasped this quickly as she found herself raising her hips, trying to hump his hand, which he managed somehow to keep always just out of range.

"Slave girls beg," he offered.

"P-Please, Master," she caught his meaning. "I need to…I need to come."

"No." The magic hand was removed. Unceremoniously, he wiped his hand on her skirt. "Sit up, slave girl."

Merrie's hand could barely operate the control. She was on the verge of tears. Trembling, feeling utterly inadequate, she tried to work the button.

"Look at me," said her temporary Master.

His gaze fixed on her, not the building afternoon traffic. "Another rule. You will suffer, you will be degraded and humiliated, but I will never leave you alone. It's a lesson for you. I will stay with you. Got it?"

She found her peace in the depthless blue field of his eyes. "Yes," she nodded, strangely reassured. "Master."

"Good. Now I want you to take off your blouse and your bra and roll your bare nipples between your fingers."

Merrie swooned. *He was going to expose her. Right here in traffic.* "B-But, Master, people will see me."

"Punishment is real," he reminded sternly. "And trust me, after three days I will know what works most effectively on you."

Merrie lowered her eyes. She had been rebuked by her Master. Her owner for the next three days. Trying not to think about the shame of it, she undid the buttons and parted the halves of her blouse. Her nipples were hot and aching, chafing the fabric of the bra. She had her hands behind her back, under the blouse to undo the strap when he stopped her.

"That's enough, slave girl. You may button your blouse back up."

She looked at him questioningly.

"Masters test their slaves," he informed her. "That too is a lesson for you to remember."

Marshall let her sit quietly for a while, giving her a chance to absorb it all. Merrie was exhausted, but she was still way over-stimulated. As if sensing her nervousness, he held her hand for a while as they drove. She had the impression that it was a subliminal act, something done under the table to counter the brittle, jarring nature of the slavery he was teaching her. Then again, that assumed the man was capable of compassion, which was as foreign to him as the ability to turn himself into a pink elephant with green spots.

Even so, she was grateful for this small human touch. For the moment, she tried to forget the three days ahead and the ordeals they might bring. Already her head was in a different space, a needy, glowing, slavish space. For while he hadn't actually made her show her tits to thousands of nearby motorists, he'd shown he could, and that was tantamount to the same thing.

Marshall took a detour before heading for the mountains. The adult toy store was located in a rundown warehouse district of the city. It was very well-stocked and neatly designed inside. She'd imagined such a place would be filled with greasy old men in raincoats, but actually there were a variety of people up and down the brightly lit aisles, including couples in their twenties and thirties.

The BDSM section was in the back of the store. Marshall explained that he could easily have left her in the car and done this himself, but he wanted her to have the experience of purchasing them. What she gained mostly was humiliation, as she was made to pick out and in some cases model the instruments he was buying to use on her hapless flesh.

Though the spike-haired clerk seemed entirely disinterested, Merrie felt that she was being exploited for both his amusement and Wilder's.

"Hold out your wrist," Marshall commanded, testing the size of the leather cuff. She drew a breath as he gathered it tight, snapping the small padlock. It was similar to the one Kennedy had given her, but under the circumstances, worlds apart.

"How does that feel?" He wanted to know, brushing her arm with the flogger, a thin leather whip-like device with a small flap of leather at the end.

"I-I don't know," she said, trying to imagine all the ways such a device might be used on a woman's body.

"I'll need rope," he changed the subject. "Nylon. Lots of it."

"We have an assortment on the far wall," said the young man in the black T-shirt.

"And handcuffs." He looked right at Meridian now. "I'll need handcuffs."

Her eyes lowered to the floor. According to him, she'd asked for this, and maybe she had, putting herself up on the Xchange. Still, it seemed to her a woman deserved better, even from a temporary Master.

"We have some excellent ones, top grade steel, made in Germany," the clerk offered.

"Good. And ankle chains, too. How about dildos and vibrators? Where can I find those?"

They had to put the items in a basket, there were so many. He had Merrie carry it, holding it out so he could add more and more things. With each selection, she became more horrified, titillated and aroused. Naming each, he held them up to her, then dropped them in with the rest. The purpose of some was painfully obvious, while others seemed more abstruse.

"Nipple clamps," he dangled the small silver chains in front of her.

A moment later, he added the large flesh-colored dildo and the butt plug. When he showed her the large strap-on mouthpiece with the plastic protrusion facing inward, she nearly fainted.

"This little beauty is a penis gag," he explained.

Merrie bit her lip. A woman, a slave girl, wearing such a device would feel like she was sucking on a rubber cock. And she would stay like that for as long as her Master wished.

As a final gesture in subjugation, he picked out lingerie for her, from among the naughty, barely there items on display. After holding up a number of items against her highly sensitized body, he settled on a white two-piece with fur-covered bra cups and a G-string.

She was close to dissolving in tears of shame when the strangest thing happened. A bearded man with a leather cap and vest and a barrel chest approached and asked Wilder if he was interested in sharing his bounties.

Marshall replied politely but firmly there would be no sharing of his woman.

"Aw, come on," rasped the biker, reaching to touch Merrie's chin. "Be a good sport and pass off the little bitch; a fine piece like this is wasted on just one guy."

Wilder moved so fast, Merrie nearly missed it.

"Apologize," he told the man as he stood behind him, pinning his arm high up his back.

The biker was facing Merrie, wincing. He never had managed to lay a hand on her.

"I'm sorry, Jeezus," he wailed to Wilder. "I was just talking."

Wilder turned him around, shoving him back. "Not about this one, you don't. She's too good for you, and don't you ever forget it."

The biker backed away, shaking out his shoulder. "You're both crazy, you know that?"

Merrie just stared at her rescuer. A show of gallantry was about the last thing she'd ever expected from the man at this point. Then again, lest she forget, it was Wilder's fault she was in this horrible store in the first place.

"If you're expecting a thank you—"

"I expect obedience," he took her by the elbow. "Nothing more. Nothing less."

Wilder made her take the items to the checkout counter herself.

"How much for the ten-inch floggers?" The gum-chewing blonde called out for a price check.

Merrie tried her best to disappear into the neon wallpaper. She thought she was going to die. The whole store, the whole world would know what she was now. Wilder's hand touched her back again, this time soothing, holding her together.

"Never mind that," he handed the girl a pair of hundred dollar bills. "Just keep the change."

The woman's eyes lit up. "Yes, sir," she whistled.

Wilder helped bag up the items and steered a dazed Merrie out the front door. Again, she wondered, was he trying to minimize her suffering? If only she could get into the man's brain, get some sense of where he was coming from. And she'd have to do so quickly, too, because the man was about to have her in his clutches for three days, alone in a mountain cabin. With her as his total slave.

It was only temporary, she told herself, and yet she had to wonder. If he could work this much magic on her already, with just a few hours here and there, what could he do with seventy-two continuous ones? The mind boggled at the possibilities.

Not to mention her quivering sex.

Chapter Five

Marshall Wilder eased the Porsche up the old dirt road. It was after ten and the moon was shining down through the T-bar roof of his classic 1978 Porsche Carrera 911. The day had been a blur and every few miles of the drive up here, he'd had to look at her to see that it was really true.

He'd kidnapped Meridian Hunter. Or was that too strong a word? He hadn't exactly held a gun to her head nor had he made any sort of threats against her. It was a mutually agreed upon submission, that was all. He had told her she would come with him to be punished, a sentence he'd quickly amended to a three-day tenure as his sex slave, and she'd gone along.

There was no mistaking what she'd gotten herself into, and by not attempting escape or offering complaint, she had given tacit consent. At least that's what he kept telling himself. Damn, his cock was so hard. Was this really all for science and logic, he asked himself, beholding the form of the sleeping woman beside him…his de facto slave girl? Was he really just trying to "cure" her of her desires?

She was lying back in the fully reclined seat at present, her body lost in the leather. She was on her side facing him, her legs curled up underneath her. Her shoes were off, which made her look even more helpless and childlike. He'd cuffed her hands in front of her for the ride up. She'd pouted for a while, but finally fallen asleep, just like a little angel.

His instinct was to gather her up now and smother her with fresh kisses. But he had to set the parameters early. This was not supposed to be a sweet, delightful experience. It was supposed to shake her up enough to make her never want to do BDSM again in her life. Still, there were limits to how he could treat her, even as her temporary Master.

"Meridian," he tapped her shoulder gently. "We're here."

"I'll have the reports…tomorrow, sir," she mumbled.

Wilder resisted a smile. Ever the hard worker. Ever the company woman. In a way he felt bad about the way it had all worked out. If he'd never made contact with her as Master Nightshade, she never would have quit. It seemed an unfair road for her to have had to walk, even if it was for her own good. Maybe he'd find something for her when this was all done. Maybe he'd even give her back her old job.

If she'd take it.

But first, the shock treatment.

"Meridian, it's time to get up. You're a slave girl, remember? I am your Master, and this is going to be your home."

For seventy-two hours at least. And agonizing hours they would be. If starting this mutual exercise between them was difficult, ending it might be a hundred times worse. Having gotten to know this woman and to enjoy her favors just once, he was already wondering if he'd be able to let her go when this was all over.

Meridian blinked, her pretty green eyes trying to focus and comprehend. She licked her lips and tried to stretch. The pull of the steel made her wince and then startle. Damn. He'd forgotten how rediscovering the cuffs might affect her waking up. Leaning down to hold her, he whispered softly in her ear.

"Don't be afraid. Remember what I told you. Master is with you. A good Master never leaves his slave."

She answered only with her eyes. Looking about her, absorbing the scene, they spoke with a dozen emotions. The cabin was set in the midst of a stand of trees, tall claw-like branches on every side, casting eerie shadows. Owls hooted in the cool night air, warning of a coming early fall. They were miles from civilization. The perfect location to enact his little scenario of temporary submission.

There was plenty she would not see until dawn. The creek where he would require her to clean herself under his inspection. The small garden, with its crop of ripened pumpkins and squash, which she would tend for him on her hands and knees. And the tree to which she could be tied and disciplined with paddle, flogger, or, if he preferred, a small switch cut from a nearby oak. Never enough to cut or seriously hurt, but enough to teach her flesh the power of his mastery.

Lastly, there was the meadow, where she would lie for him, amidst the tall grass and the flowers, her body furrowed by his manhood for as long as his heart desired.

He set her down on her feet on the porch, just outside the front door. "You'll have to enter the house naked," he said gently, moving in front of her to undo the handcuffs.

The poor thing was still half-asleep and weak as a kitten, but the principle was very important. The slave did not enter the Master's house clothed, least of all with any garments she'd bought herself. It was she who was the property now and any covering she had, she'd get from him, by his largesse.

"I'm f-freezing," she whispered, though he knew it was more a state of mind than anything else.

Excusing the fact that she wasn't calling him Master for the moment, he said, "I'll light a fire inside. You can lie in front of it, on the rug."

Indeed, he had plans for her on that great surface of bearskin, plans which would warm her little body quickly enough.

Merrie stood and undressed, handing over the blouse, bra and skirt. Wilder's blood raced at the sight of the curvy little submissive standing before him in only her panties. It brought back memories, of other women, other scenes. The temptation was great to draw out her suffering, to make her beg to come inside. To require her to take his cock into her mouth as a self-offering first. But he must go slowly. She was new to this, he couldn't forget. It was a fine line, shocking her into giving up BDSM while not really causing any harm to her sweet and innocent person.

"Take off your panties," he said. "Kneel and offer them to me."

"C-Cold," she whispered.

"It will be all right," he soothed. "You can do this."

He'd been in this place before, too. Yearning to push a woman harder, but at the same time getting off on the tenderness, too, the power exercised in the form of gentle mercy, enjoying the woman's response, her body soft, grateful and orgasmic. There were purists who said this could not be done effectively when love was there to confuse things, but Marshall had never been able to do this without loving a woman.

Present company excluded, of course. He could not, must not love Meridian Hunter. That would only trap her and confuse her, and ultimately, doom them both.

She slipped the little pink garment down over her hips, her flanks pale and luminescent in the moonlight. He clenched his fists, watching her. It was a tremulous and tentative but very real act of obedience. Meridian Hunter was doing as she was told, and she would continue to, slaking his every desire for three straight days.

The panties fell to her slim ankles. One by one she lifted her bare feet off the wooden porch floor. She was naked now. A moment later, she dropped to the wood, gingerly on tender kneecaps, proffering the underwear.

He allowed her to remain like this, for a precious few seconds, subservient, looking up at him, offering her most personal garment, and with it, her unplumbed sexual depths. Soon, very soon, he would know them and her, better than any man on the planet. It was all he could do not to embrace her, to kiss away all of this emotion he knew was inside her. To put her at ease and then to have his way with her, at a level, a depth no two people could ever understand without dominance and submission.

"Things will happen," he said impulsively. "Between us. You must trust me in all of it. Do you understand?"

"Yes, Master." She whispered. Her pliant voice fanning the flames of his Dominant desires even more.

"When we get inside," he told her, noting how the mountain air had turned her nipples to bullets. "You will forget everything but pleasing me. Just like when we were online. Only now it will be real. Is that clear?"

She nodded, a complexity of emotions upon her submissive face. "Yes, Master."

A small frown darkened his face. There was no way it could all be clear in her mind. She hadn't a clue what this would do to her. And come to think of it, neither did he. Playing with her in cyberspace was one thing. But here, in the flesh, could be something very different.

Uncharted territory is what it was, and there was only one way to find out where it might take them. Wilder opened the door to the cabin. It creaked loudly.

"Crawl," he instructed, indicating that she should cross the threshold on all fours.

The sight of the woman down like this was almost more than he could bear. It would take all his willpower not to convey her to the bearskin rug and have his way with her, filling her pussy immediately. Or else to slide himself between her other lips and come at the first thrust.

The cabin was damp and dark. Merrie clung to his leg as soon as he closed the door. He could hear the beginnings of sobs. Once again, he would have to accommodate the weakness of her flesh, of her femininity. Cradling her in his arms, he carried her to the brass bed on the far wall of the one-room cabin.

"Wait here," he tucked her under the comforters, a triple layer of goose down. "Until I get the fire going."

She looked up at him with small, appreciative eyes. "Yes, Master. Thank you, Master."

He scowled, knowing that look on her face all too well. The romance of slavery, the thrill a woman feels when first she begins to live out fantasies she has only dreamt of before. It would be his job to show her that the reality fell terribly short and that no woman could possibly crave in real life what she sought in dreams.

Again, it would be his lesson that would save her from making some dread mistake with another, less scrupulous man.

"You may not speak," he told her, "unless spoken to."

Enjoying a brief respite from the nonstop arousal he'd felt since encountering her trying to vandalize his car, he selected the pieces of wood from the bin one by one, arranged them artfully in the fireplace, then lit them with one carefully placed match.

In no time at all there was a crackling, roaring fire in the hearth, enough to raise the cabin temperature a good five degrees in a matter of minutes. Making sure the windows were cracked for ventilation, Wilder shed his jacket and shirt, stripping down to his bare chest. Turning back to the bed now, he beheld his small, wide-eyed prize.

It was time for her real lessons to begin.

Pulling down the covering, he exposed her small naked form. His to do with as he willed.

"Sleeping in a bed is a privilege for a slave," he explained. "As is everything else in her life. Kneel," he snapped his fingers, pointing to a place beside his feet. "Here."

Merrie lowered herself to the floor. Her technique and posture was amateurish, but held great potential. He went to fetch the riding crop. It was the kind with a flap on the end, tightly stitched. She watched in trepidation as he fetched it, her eyes glued to his every action.

"When you kneel for your Master," he returned to face her, "you must sit back on your heels."

She shuddered, just a bit as he tapped her milk-white thigh with the end of the crop. Down went her buttocks, digging into her heels.

"And your thighs must be wide apart. Always wide. As much as you can manage."

Merrie sighed. He knew the effect this was having on her. He could smell it, too, raw liquid submission.

"Wider," he commanded, tapping her again.

"This," he ran the leather flap over her fully exposed sex, "is the Master's property. You may never hide it from him."

"Oh, M-Master," she moaned as he pressed the device directly against her clit.

Wilder administered a stinging corrective to her thigh. "Were you given permission to speak?"

She shook her head no, shock evident on her face. It was not a particularly painful blow, but it was no doubt the first one she'd ever felt in her life, outside of her own fantasies.

"Head up," he lifted her chin, again employing the device that was now an extension of his own arm, not to mention his will. "Back straight."

The slave was afraid of how this angle would expose her breasts, and rightly so.

"Hands behind your head," he said sternly. "Push your nipples towards me. No matter what, you may not break position."

Her breathing was quick and excited. A few judicious touches and she would be writhing on the floor in orgasm. Never in his life had he seen such responses to a man's commands.

"Do you know what the worst torture of being a slave is?" Casually, cruelly, he flicked her left nipple with the crop.

"No, Master," she panted, nearly swooning.

"It's not the lack of freedom or having your body owned, as you might think." Wilder did the same to the other nipple. It was taking all she had to keep herself still, allowing him to play with her like this. "No, in actuality, it's the fact that your desires, your responses are owned, as well. You must be wet and aroused and even have orgasms simply because it pleases your Master to see you in that state. Just as he might at another time enjoy watching you cheer at a football game or scrub the floors on your hands and knees. But most of all, the Master gets off on teasing you. Making you beg."

He rubbed both nipples in turn now, taking his time with the crop to create a line of pleasure down her spine. In a few seconds, he had her torso undulating.

"You were told to remain still," he slapped her left breast with the crop.

Chastened, the slave went rigid, red-faced.

"This is what you exist for," he refocused her, cupping his aching cock and balls through his trousers. "To tantalize and satisfy your Master."

He ought to have spent more time training her to respond to the crop, but he could wait no longer to feel her mouth on him. Undoing his zipper, he pulled out the rock-hard shaft that would no longer be contained.

"Keep your hands behind your head," he said. "And I will teach you how to suck a man's cock properly."

Meridian's lips were half-open. She looked up at him in awe.

"This," he ran his hand along the over-sensitive shaft, "is your touchstone and guide in life as a slave. It directs your life, in many fundamental ways, and you must never forget that it is this piece of flesh that you serve. You must be creative and diligent. Your whole being is made to please your Master's cock—remember that when you are attending to it with your mouth. A Master knows the difference as she is fellating him, if his slave has that depth of understanding and obedience or not."

He was within a hairsbreadth of her full, feminine lips. The pretty, clever lips that could nearly outwit him in the boardroom. Lips that would now learn their place.

"You may kiss the head of my cock, slave girl."

Her face was slack with desire, the lips puffy and full of arousal. It was like the touch of a flower, petals completely open. It was this moment he never failed to relish as a Master. Having the slave surrendered, her heart and belly in full anticipation, unable to clench or resist in any way, even though his taking of her might well be full, even harsh.

"Look at it, slave girl."

Wilder's shaft was pounding with blood, the veins raised, thick with pulsing life. A drop of pre-come peeked from out of the head of it. She seemed duly impressed, duly excited.

"Taking your Master's cock is also a privilege. Do you understand?"

"Yes, Master," she replied, lightly panting and fully awed.

Wilder put his hands on his hips imperiously. "You may beg to suck, slave girl."

"Mmmm," she sighed, her voice sexy as hell. "I beg you, Master. Please, may I suck your cock?"

"Lick it first, show me what you can do."

She did not have to be told how to use her tongue. At one point he'd thought this a natural skill in all women, but he'd since learned there were many who lacked it, or blocked it out. Jenifer had sent him to the moon with her oral skills, until they'd sealed the marriage vows, then it all went to hell. If he could manage to flog himself twenty-four-seven for not signing a prenuptial agreement with that woman, he'd arrange it. It was his dominant Master's vanity that had held him back. He'd imagined their bond and his power over her to be stronger than anything on the planet.

In the end, though, greed overrides everything. And the need to survive. This is what Merrie needed to learn. Exploit or be exploited. That was the human condition.

"Slave girls must be exquisitely pleasing," he ran his hand over the top of her hair, silky red and beautiful. "There is no room for excuse, or margin for error. If the Master isn't satisfied, the slave can expect a whipping or any other punishment he may devise. And a man won't tell you up front, Meridian, what he is going to do to you. A naïve little woman like you could sign up for an easy bondage and end up chained in someone's basement, eating from a dog dish and servicing all his friends. You think that doesn't happen with Xchange.com?"

Wilder clasped the sides of her head. He needed her more than he'd ever needed anything in his life.

"Just…relax your jaws," he grunted. He was afraid to push her too far, too fast, but to his surprise, she more than met him half-way. In fact, she was like a hungry little vacuum tube, taking him deep to the back of her throat.

Damn. Was this talk of abusive slavery turning her on?

"This...isn't a game," he tried to keep in didactic mode despite his arousal. "You and I...are playing nice here...some men...don't play...they hurt."

Merrie's head bobbed up and down in perfect submission. There was not the slightest hesitation, not the slightest reluctance. Somehow his plan was failing, miserably.

"That's enough," he pushed her away. "You will crawl onto the rug by the fire, facing it, ass in the air, breasts down. You will put your left cheek to the fur, place your hands behind you and use your fingers to spread your buttocks cheeks. You will hold that position until told otherwise."

Meridian licked her lips. Her eyes were soft and doe-like, but behind them was a new light, as if something were dawning on her, deep and profound. "Yes," she said softly, her voice sweet balm to his grated nerves. "Master."

Wilder poured himself a scotch from the cabinet above the counter in the kitchen area. Leaning against it, he regarded the prostrate woman. Vice President for Creative Development, Meridian Hunter, one of the most capable females he'd ever encountered, and by far the most challenging.

Jeezus, he thought as he swallowed the aged, well-browned liquid, *what have I gotten myself into? This woman has let me lead her down this trail, and I have no idea where the other end will come out. Here she is, in the most abject position possible, her intimacies totally exposed to me, calmly awaiting whatever I might dish out.*

And it could be anything. Even he wasn't sure. A paddling? A down and dirty fuck? The thought even crossed his mind to take her in the ass. Whatever he did, it would have to follow the game plan of keeping one step ahead of her. So far she was calling his bluff. She was a tough cookie—that shouldn't surprise him. But he had to break her. In the nicest way possible.

In fact, he had to get her to beg him to end the experiment. Cry uncle. And it had to be soon, too, because at this rate, he might end up having to fold his hand before she did.

*****

Meridian felt just like a slave from out of one of her fantasies as she presented her ass to her Master. Naked, offering her nude body as a pretty little diversion on a giant fur rug. The fact that she was arrayed like this on top of a grizzly's skin only made it the more deliciously wicked. She knew from the articles she'd read that Wilder was a hunter. Had he bagged this beast himself? He never used a gun, only a crossbow, he had said in the interview. More sporting that way.

She heard the gurgling behind her, the sound of Wilder pouring liquid into a glass. A fresh wave of surrender spasmed her pussy. He was the Master, helping himself to a drink, and she was the slave, forced to wait to receive whatever beverage he might choose. What would it be like, she wondered, to live like this all the time? And with a man like him, no less? What if she really did have to beg for food and clothing? What if he treated her more strictly even than a child?

And what about the sex? What would it be like to have to perform, to spread and come and suck on command, just because it gave him his jollies? It was a disgusting, demeaning thought, one that cut against everything society had taught her. So why did it make her yearn so much and why did it make her heart soar like no other idea in her life?

Meridian was confused. She was a person. She had plans. To run Wilder's new company. To maybe marry and have children one day with a good, loving, equal man. So why did she want, at the same time, to be a toy like this, the most degraded of sex objects? She ought to get up. Grab for her clothes. Demand he take her home. Steal his car keys. Whatever it took. Nothing was keeping her here. He wouldn't really restrain her, he'd said as much. So what was going on, really?

Maybe she wanted to beat him at his own game. Prove she could take it all and ask for more. Yes, that was it. Meridian Hunter liked the challenge of it. And in the end, she would win. Wilder would throw up his hands and admit he couldn't control her. Or presume to understand and satisfy her sexual needs.

Merrie tensed at the sound of approaching shoe leather. It was amazing how sensitive she was like this, down here on the floor. She was so utterly dependent now. Every muscle tensed. Would he touch her? Whip her?

"Among the many things you do not realize, slave girl," Wilder said, not laying a finger on her…yet. "Is that the vast majority of men regard the opposite gender as a commodity. Nearly three-quarters of the world's women serve in some form of bondage, did you know that? There are the outright slaves, who are openly chained and branded throughout much of the Third World, the brothel slaves, hidden away in basements and high rises in every city on earth from Akron to Amman, the sweat shop girls and farm and factory slaves, and then there are the so-called wives, who are the property of their husbands in most places, even in this enlightened century. Americans are woefully naïve, I assure you, of what things are really like on this planet. Have you any clue how many women, even our own, are lost to the white slave trade each year? Just one more thing to think about, when you play about on the Xchange, flashing your pretty backside…Miss ownmenow."

His tongue was a little looser. She detected the odor of scotch. He'd had a drink of alcohol. Her belly clenched, her person so totally at his mercy.

"Place your arms in front of you, slave girl. Extend your hands, palm down towards the fire. Stretch yourself fully, while remaining on your knees."

The new position made her feel like she was prostrating herself before a god. Except this god was behind her.

"I told you that you would be punished," he reminded, tapping the crop here and there on her tightly stretched ass cheeks. "You have a lovely ass for a slave, do you know that?"

The crop whistled in the air before landing smartly on her skin.

"You may thank Master for the compliment."

The sting was diffuse, the sensation more erotic than it was painful. "Thank you, Master," she exclaimed.

"Once whipped, a woman is different," he remarked. "She becomes truly a slave."

He struck her again, eliciting a moan. It could scarce have been more intimate an action than if he had been penetrating her with his sex.

"You redden nicely…slave girl."

"T-Thank you, Master." Merrie took her whipping as best she was able. It had begun to hurt and she was getting frustrated, too, as she was feeling deep need in her pussy that cried out to be satisfied. Ashamed of her own desires, she began to lift her buttocks higher, needing more.

"What would you like now, slave girl?" asked her Master after the tenth blow.

It was as if he'd read her mind.

"I-I need your cock, Master."

"You may beg for it," he offered magnanimously.

Her mouth was parched. She doubted she would have the air to speak. "I…please," she whimpered, rubbing her belly and breasts against the bearskin. "Please…take me."

"You will beg to be fucked," he laid the crop across her exposed pussy lips. "Like the pleasure-giving animal that you are."

Was that really what she was—an animal…for sex?

Merrie's pussy clenched in anticipation. "Oh, god…Master…my Master…fuck me…fuck your slave girl…please…"

"Will you be a good lay for Master?"

His words came back to her now, from the car. The slave girl is allowed no pride.

"Yes," she gobbled up the humiliation, craving it nearly as much as the fucking itself. "I will…I will try to be good…for Master."

"You are in my power," he reminded her. "If you do not please me, I can, if I wish, leave you outside for the night."

"Ohh…Master," she moaned, the cruel strength of his words wrapping her like hot steel chains.

Would he really do that? Would he really treat her so cruelly? It didn't matter, just saying it, just pretending even, was enough to send her sailing.

"Please, Master, fuck your slave girl…let her please you…let her…earn the right to sleep inside."

God, what was she saying? Worse still, how badly would she hate herself in the morning? She could hear him undressing, the subtle sound of the metal zipper, the sound of his clothes hitting the floor. She lived for every little motion. His naked body would be coming to her, soon, very soon.

Wilder showed no mercy this time. As soon as he had hold of her hips, he thrust himself home. One deep, satisfying push and he had sunk himself to the hilt. "Mine," he declared without the least bit of shame.

"M-Master," she cried, digging her nails into the rug.

"You will come with me," he said calmly, as though discussing some business matter. "At the same moment as me. Or else I might just let you spend the night shackled to a tree."

"Yes," she grunted, dragging the word out into long syllables. "Yes…Master."

She concentrated with every fiber of her being on what he was doing to her. She was right there, ready to explode, but she had to hold back…the same time as him, that's what he had said.

And to think with her other lovers she had just lain there, letting them pump her, praying for them to get it over with, going through the motions of a phony orgasm just to get them off her faster.

"Was it good for you, baby?" they'd croon.

"Oh, you know it, lover," she'd lie to them sweet as pie.

Blah. Blah. Blah. Just waiting until she could be alone and masturbate to scenes like this. Scenes of being ravished by a man totally in control, calling all the shots and demanding she be along for the ride.

"Is that what does it for you?" he mocked, his voice a low growl as he noticed the fresh flood of juices. "Hearing me talk about chaining you to the pine tree all night? You want to try it for real? Hell, you don't have it in you to endure that kind of punishment," he scorned. "You wouldn't make it five minutes. Give it up, woman. Admit it's too much. Just say the words, and I'll drive you home, right now, no questions asked."

"Never," she groaned. "Master."

Wilder let out a deep sigh, like he'd been stabbed. The sperm shot from him, hot and deep. Merrie cried out in joy, clutching his cock, the muscles of her pussy magnifying his pleasure with her own climax. Never before had she so fully understand what an orgasm meant for her; how it was all about making it sweeter for the man inside her. Where once she'd felt so childish and even guilty for not enjoying pleasuring herself as much as her girlfriends in college, now she understood what that was all about.

Her body was made for a man to have. She could find no real joy in sex without that. But what kind of man was she made for? And would that man have to be a Master?

Wilder said no, but what did he know? He was the least able to judge her of anyone in the world. He knew nothing of her, he cared not at all for her and he took every opportunity to prove it.

"Turn around, slave girl." Her Master smacked her ass, pulling her back from her post-orgasmic reverie into her captive reality. "Lick me clean."

Her breath caught in her throat. He wanted her to clean his cock, to wipe it of their sex juices using...her tongue. No self-respecting, twenty-first century woman would do such a thing.

"Now, slave."

"Ow, stop it," she cried over her shoulder. This time he had spanked her hard.

Wilder brought her to heel, his finger hooking just beneath her clitoris. In seconds he had her moaning, in heat all over again. Instead of giving relief, he made it ache maddeningly. "What did you say to me, Meridian?"

"Nothing, Master. I didn't mean anything."

He kept her dangling, raw on the edge of another climax, giving proof to what he'd said about a slave's body belonging not to herself but to the Master.

"Tell me what you want," he prompted.

Merrie was identifying the pattern already. What she must want, what she must do was obey. "I want to lick your cock clean, Master."

He withdrew his finger carefully, denying her an orgasm. "Do it."

She scrambled in a circle, miserably, on hands and knees. She found him standing now, his penis hardly diminished. Such a sight it was, as it glistened in the warm firelight, covered with her juices and his. God, she really did want to do this after all. She was actually hungry for it, for the taste of him all over again. And for the chance to serve as an end in itself, doing this humble little thing for him. Why did she feel like she belonged here? Why was it so…right?

"In a little while I am going to take a nap," he told her, allowing her to continue lapping at his cock long after the sex juices were gone. "You will cook me something to eat. Use the groceries in the car, and wake me when it's ready."

She was about to ask what groceries, when he seized her by the hair and pushed her mouth back over his reinvigorated shaft. "You will swallow it," he said. "Every drop."

Meridian took her Master's cock deep. He was going to come in her mouth—it was his will and she had no choice. How long she had craved this kind of decisiveness from her male partners. Each and every time they'd been overwhelmed by her squeamishness. Hadn't they known this was what she needed? To be forced to follow her own secret desires? To have a man override all her negative social conditioning about what good girls should and shouldn't do?

Merrie was amazed at his resiliency. He was no less hard now than before. And he'd had almost no recovery time between erections, either. How many times a day did a man like this come? She thought of yet another statement of his, how a slave has to live to serve her Master's penis. Watching it, pleasing it, knowing that it is what she's built for. Was that supposed to turn her off? Quite the opposite. For the right man, what wouldn't she give in the way of sexual pleasing? She'd worship a cock all right, so long as it was the one and only cock, the one attached to her mate for life.

If such an elusive creature as that could ever exist for her.

Tentatively, hoping it wouldn't violate one of his many rules, Merrie put her hands on his buttocks. The flesh was lean, strong, with not an ounce of fat. She felt even more his subject as she pressed her own soft palms against him. Again she thought of the rightness of all of this.

Wilder didn't seem to mind her improvisation. He was preoccupied, getting himself off. He was more lax this time, letting her do all the work. A single hand on top of her head, petting and caressing was as far as he was going to orchestrate the act.

"That's a good slave, Merrie," he murmured, applying the diminutive of her name—usually reserved for her friends.

She felt born in that sound—as if no one had ever pronounced her name before. She called his in turn, but the articulation was lost in her deep suctioning. One or two more grunts, low and guttural, and the man was coming down her throat. She swallowed and swallowed, her first time since college she'd done such a thing, and then it had been on a dare, after consuming the better part of an entire bottle of tequila.

"Angel," he whispered softly.

Merrie wilted at the new tone. Putting her head against his thigh, she just relished the moment. She should have been outraged, but she wasn't; she'd pleased her Master and it felt...right. It was complicated, she decided, this slavery thing.

"Master," she murmured.

"I want my supper," he tugged on the back of her hair. "You will commence cooking it. There's all you need in the car. I stopped at the store while you were sleeping."

Merrie felt the stirrings of rebellion. "You expect me to get them myself…Master…now?"

"What's the matter?" He smirked. "Scared of the dark? Or is it the bogeyman you're worried about?"

Her green eyes narrowed. "Not at all. I'm sure any monsters out there won't be nearly as disgusting as the one in here."

He smiled, seemingly amused at her display. "You may wear my jacket," he offered her the suit coat.

"How gentlemanly of you."

Wilder put it over her shoulders, using the opportunity to kiss her neck. Merrie turned away as best she could, but as usual, it was impossible to resist the man. "I hate you," she let him know. "Master."

"I know," he soothed, draping his hands to play with her nipples. "That's what makes it more fun."

She fell back against him, all thoughts of rebellion and dinner and everything else gone. "Master, please, can we…"

Wilder pulled back. "No," he pushed her forward, his palm tapping her naked ass. "We can't. I want sleep and dinner. Run along. I'll watch from the door to make sure you don't get eaten by anything too nasty on the way."

Ooh, this man drove her crazy. He was a total bully, a complete…well, slave driver. Then again, he was looking after her just like he said. And as scary as it was to walk out to the car in the moonlight, barely clothed, she knew deep down he would never let any harm come to her. It was this last thought, this odd combination of being stripped down to the bone and yet supremely cherished that puzzled her most. It wasn't a fantasy thing, not like in her dreams of dungeons and mighty lords. No, this was something else, something heady, confusing, and almost mystical.

Was it unique to Wilder or would she find it with any man before whom she stripped and begged and sucked abjectly? She sure as hell hoped so, because the thought of spending even a minute with Wilder past the three days filled her with the deepest dread of her life.

A lump formed in her throat as she stood on the pine needle-covered ground, rummaging in the trunk for the bags. What was it Kennedy had said? Hate was just another four-letter word, like lust and love?

It took her two trips to get all four of the paper sacks. Each was overfull, with various items, from tall stalks of celery and packaged mushrooms to thick, juicy steaks. There were also breakfast staples, some peanut butter and jam, several kinds of bread and a bottle of French red wine.

Wilder closed the door behind her on the second trip. "No dawdling," he told her, like she was an errant child. "And no nibbling, either. If I find you've eaten so much as one bite of anything, I'll paddle your behind redder than the tomatoes. Got it?"

"Yes," she swallowed her pride, for the umpteenth time. "Master."

"Good. And unless you want that little sperm deposit I gave your tummy to be your only supper, you'd better cook up something tasty."

Merrie fumed, thankful he wasn't expecting an answer. How dare the man talk to her like this! It was one thing in the middle of sex, to spice things up, but this was…real life. Totally different.

Setting the last two bags on the counter, she began to pull out the items, mindlessly. Robotically, going through the motions, she found herself chopping onions with a large knife. A big enough knife to cut his balls off, she thought grimly. And what was to stop her?

The bastard was snoring. She was sure she could pull it off.

The nerve, leaving her naked, to cook for him, telling her she wouldn't eat unless she did a good job. Taunting her with the fact that she'd already "eaten", taking down his hot, salty sperm.

But what did she expect? She was a slave. That was the deal. Merrie felt between her legs. She was still dripping. Her nipples were still hard as pebbles. God, but she needed relief. He'd said she couldn't eat, but what about masturbating? Okay, orgasms weren't supposed to be allowed, but when it came right down to it, how would he ever know?

Slipping her hands between her legs, she touched herself. The rush was instantaneous, and immediately the world was lost to her. So much so that she failed to notice that he had stopped snoring, and had in fact come up behind her.

He grasped her wrist, his grip as firm as steel. "Game over, my beauty. You lose."

Meridian felt the world drop from underneath her. The man had come out of nowhere, naked, stone-faced, and looking none too pleased.

"Marshall," she gasped, then quickly correcting herself. "Master, I can explain."

"Explain?" He laughed dryly. "I think the situation speaks for itself, don't you?"

"I was just cooking," she lied foolishly.

Marshall spun her about with ease, lifting the evidence to his nostrils. "Yes, you were cooking, all right, but not my food."

She flushed red.

"Taste," he ordered. "Tell me what flavor this is."

Merrie whimpered, but relented under his withering gaze. "It's...me," she whispered, putting the tips of her glistening fingers to her lips, her tongue dabbing shyly.

"Be more specific," he demanded.

Merrie felt the heat spread down her chest. If his intent was humiliation, he was doing a good job. "It's...my come," she said. "From my pussy."

"Lick it off."

Merrie's knees went weak. She had never done such a thing in her life. Seeing his resolve, however, she relented, cleaning her fingers thoroughly under his supervision. The taste was tangy, elementally female. And if he wanted more, there was plenty to be had right now, fresh and fragrant between her legs.

"Were you given permission to play with yourself, slave girl?"

"No, Master."

"What do you think should be done with you?"

Merrie's chest rose and fell rapidly as she contemplated the possibilities. Her nipples were tight bullets. She was sopping wet, and all too aware of his hard, naked body, just inches from hers, preventing her escape.

"I should be…punished," she breathed, the words sending slow, lazy shockwaves down her spine, weakening her nearly to the point of collapse.

Marshall flipped her damp curls over her shoulders with deceptive gentleness. "You're a very pretty woman, Meridian, but you're undisciplined. As a genuine slave you would be found very wanting."

She shuddered at the brush of his fingertips across her earlobes to her lips. "I want to be better, Master."

He let her lick and suck at his fingers, showing just how much she wanted to improve. Greedily, she took them deep, casting a longing glance at him. She wanted his hands on her body so badly that she'd do anything to get that right now.

She needed him, too, pawing her breasts, manhandling between her legs, using and taking her. But it was not her place to ask. She had no rights any longer. She was his, a play-toy to do with as he wished.

Desperately, she tried to slip to her knees.

"No," he said, his fingers under her chin holding her up. "It's not that easy this time. Run and get me the penis gag from the bag of toys."

"Yes, Master." Merrie's feet padded across the floor. Just the friction of her thighs rubbing, slick with her own liquids, was almost enough to make her come. It was all she could do to keep herself together enough to fetch it and hand it over.

It was so exciting, every little moment, every little action, every little bit of control he was exercising. It wound her tighter and tighter.

"Open," he commanded.

The gag was rubber and slid cleanly over her tongue, filling her from the roof of her mouth out to her cheeks. True to its name, it was a simulated cock so that, when he secured the straps behind her head, Merrie found herself performing mandatory fellatio.

In order to keep the spittle in her mouth circulating she had either to swallow, or to drool through the tiny recesses in the side.

"Many slaves wear these hours at a time," he said, pulling her hair out from under the straps.

She looked at him longingly. Merrie wanted his real cock, not a substitute. Then again she'd broken the rules and now she was being punished.

Marshall handled both her breasts expertly, one in each hand. "The thing you have yet to grasp, the real difference between fantasy and reality, is that in your dreams, men do what you like to make you feel good, even if that means ravishing you. But in reality, Masters do what they like, whether or not it turns you on."

Merrie begged with her eyes. She needed an orgasm, any way she could get it.

"Bend over," he said. "And touch your toes."

She thought he might fuck her this way, but after caressing her pussy for just a few seconds, he removed his hand. She was drooling, the spittle forming a tiny line down her cheek.

Marshall touched her again, this time resting his palm on her ass. She jolted, as if he had hit her.

"Jittery little thing," he teased pulling back his hand in preparation.

Meridian nearly fell over with the impact, a heavy smack, flesh on flesh. She had just been spanked. He did it again, confirming the reality of her punishment.

"A slave girl's training can be harsh," he said. "And excruciating." His finger trailed over her clit, making her moan into the gag. Before she could climax, however, he smacked her again. Twice more he alternated, pleasure and pain before finally finishing her off.

"Come," he ordered, his finger on her pulsing clitoris.

She pushed her palms against the floor, rocking her body, like some kind of she-beast. All shame gone, she gave into the sensations, her overheated behind jiggling enticingly.

"Get up," he said at last. "It's time to get you into something a little less comfortable."

*****

Wilder chewed slowly, savoring each morsel. The freshly spanked slave girl was at his feet, chained on her knees, ankle to wrist, hands behind her back, watching the progress of his fork. Miserably, her head and eyes followed the journey of each little piece of the porterhouse he'd ended up preparing himself. Her head bobbing behavior amused him because it was very like that of a dog, though this particular creature was infinitely more complex and interesting.

So far she'd been allowed two bites, by dint of begging, the gag having been removed earlier for feeding purposes. He couldn't imagine it had done much to take the edge off her hunger, and he was quite sure she would plead just as eagerly the next time he allowed her the opportunity to open her saucy mouth.

Twice, after putting her into her current state of bondage, he'd asked if she'd had enough. She'd said she hadn't, that she wanted to go on. Things were getting a little bit heavy-duty now—subjugating her in chains and depriving her of food. The fact that this—along with her earlier punishment for masturbating—turned her on did not bode well for the future of the experiment. In fact, he was seriously considering calling the whole thing off, throwing in the towel before something happened that might mark her permanently, spoiling her for freedom, as the saying went.

Trouble was, he was enjoying the hell out of the game himself.

"Would the little slave like another bite?"

"Yes, please," said the much demeaned slave girl with what sounded to be utter sincerity. "The slave begs another bite from her Master."

He waved the fork in front of his mouth for a moment and then ate the newly speared piece himself. "And what will the slave do in exchange for more meat?"

"Anything, Master. I seek only to please you."

His heart revved several notches. She was probably just playing up to him and even if she wasn't, she had no idea what she was saying—not really. Still, the fantasy was there, these being the words that every dominant male longs to hear all his life, from a flesh and blood woman. The right woman, that is.

"You think you know how to please me?" He picked the vibrator up off the table, one of several toys he'd set aside for her torture. "You haven't a clue."

He reached down, resting it between her legs. Slowly, he moved it back and forth, again and again, each time nearly to the opening of her sex only to pull it back. He waited until she was clenching, wanting it desperately. Finally, he gave it to her, sinking it all the way in.

"Don't let it fall out," he warned, turning the device onto a low buzz setting.

Meridian moaned, clenching the little automated fucking device inside her. In a matter of minutes, she would be out of her mind with uncontrolled orgasms.

Wilder pulled his chair back from the table and turned it sideways to face her. He was naked himself, sporting a huge erection, bigger than anything he'd seen in a decade. Even with Jenifer, on a good day.

"Wine?" He held the glass to her lips.

His slave's face showed sweet pain. She was locked in ecstasy, amazed at what her body could do, what he could make her feel. Obediently she parted her lips. He touched the glass to them just as the first orgasm swept her, a little punching one, wormed out of her by the whirring, insidious little device. Her lips trembled as she moaned, causing the wine to dribble down her neck, over her exposed breasts and down her belly.

Wilder stroked his cock in satisfaction, absorbing the sight of her, the sweet sounds of enforced pleasure, the smell of seduction mixed with pungent wine and bittersweet mushroom sauce.

"Open wide." He had a piece of meat between his fingers. The slave took it from him, greedily, like a little bird. She was coming again, and he helped her along, turning her nipple ever so slightly between his thumb and forefinger.

The slave girl chewed as best she could, teeth chattering, eyes rolling. Her body was straining in every direction against the chains. She wanted it all at once. The food, his touch, more wine, more orgasms. But above all, she wanted simply to be, to melt into his reality, so she could become his desire, mold herself to his need without it ever having to go through her separate person at all.

In a sudden, wanton impulse, he poured wine over her breast and bent to suckle it.

"Master," she cried, the word coming out of her mouth with such conviction, he nearly believed her.

But it couldn't be. He told himself that as he continued to masturbate. It was a game. A lesson. An exercise. And whatever other bullshit names he wanted to give it. Damn, he wanted himself inside her and not that silly little vibrator.

But this time he was going to hold firm. He was going to break her. For her own good. And then he was going to heal her, and send her on her way. A few hours older and a hell of a lot wiser.

"What's to stop me from bringing other men up here?" He wanted to know, placing the delicate silver clamps on her wine-soaked breasts. "What's to stop me from giving the use of your body to anyone I choose, any and all orifices? One after another, or maybe two at once, one in your mouth and one from behind. Is there anything you can do to prevent that…slave?"

"Nothing, Master." Meridian's torso contorted in response. From his own self-experiments he knew the pain she was feeling to be both excruciating and maddeningly sexual.

"Nothing at all, you're right," he concurred, making sure they were tight enough. "And mark my words, a real Master, the kind you find on the Xchange will do that to you. You'll be loaned out, played with en masse, swapped, potentially even sold."

"I would be a real slave," she moaned in acknowledgement, coming yet again.

"Were you given permission for any of these orgasms?" He demanded, tugging on the chain that held together the clamps.

She looked at him in anguish, realizing the trap she'd been put into. "No, Master," she shivered, her face awash in uncontrollable sensation. "Oh, Master, please…what is…happening to me?"

"You are being a disobedient slave," he said coldly. "That is what is happening."

"I'm sorry," she whimpered, sounding more afraid of disappointing him than of being punished.

He frowned. Another bad sign. She was forming an emotionally submissive attachment. "Eat." He pushed another bit of steak between her lips.

She worked on the piece while another orgasm overtook her. God, how beautiful she looked this way, his vanquished angel.

"I'm surprised at you," he took a different tack, removing the clamps. "A woman as smart as you, being so easily manipulated."

She looked at him, her face lost in panting wonder. How many layers did this woman have, anyway?

"I'm sorry," she breathed. "Master."

"Put your head back."

She did so and he poured the rest of the glass of wine over her breasts, making sure to center the flow over each throbbing, swollen nipple. The liquid sluiced downwards from there, drenching her thighs and pussy. "Thank me," he said, "for spilling wine on you."

She repeated the words with such conviction as to make him want to fuck her mouth. But it was time for something else. And he was pretty sure the mere mention of it would be enough to send her running to the hills, and off of Xchange.com for life.

"A slave's body is not her own, do you remember I told you that?"

She took the meat he was giving, nibbling gently. "Yes, Master."

"A real Master would use you not only in your pussy and mouth but in your ass as well. You understand that?"

She shook her head yes.

"Then that is what I am going to do to you. Unless you want to concede."

The slave looked at him, perplexed. "I am a virgin there, Master."

He smiled, relief flooding him. It was over. And not a moment too soon. "I'll get you cleaned up," he rose to his feet. "We'll head back now and be in the city by dawn."

"Master, no," she cried. "Don't give up on me."

Somehow she had managed to push herself forward enough to reach his leg and kiss it. Incredible. The woman was like iron. Wilder clenched his fists.

"Meridian, for god's sake. Have you not had enough of this? Isn't it clear where all of this is leading? Do you really want to become the kind of woman who lives to be controlled and dominated?"

She grew quiet against him, and a moment later he heard her sobbing.

Wonderful, now she was going to get emotional on him. At once he felt the stab of guilt. He'd been careless to treat her like this. She was a novice, and as he'd told her himself, this was not just a game, but potentially something deeply life-altering.

All thoughts of fucking her in the ass, driving her home or otherwise being at odds with her vanished from his head. For the moment at least, he must give her comfort, restore her sense of balance. What was it, anyway, that made all this so confusing? The more he tried to simplify her life the more he seemed to jumble it up.

"Meridian, I'm sorry." Stooping down, he undid the locks on her chains.

"Y-You hate me," she was crying, the words coming in single, punctuated stabs. "I'm a…terrible slave."

It was a counter-reaction she was going through, a sudden emotional release resulting from a long, intense period of trying to obey another's will.

"Shh," he calmed her, lifting her to her feet and gathering her into his arms. "You're not a terrible slave and I don't hate you. I'm just showing you that this life is wrong for you, that's all."

Her wet body pressed to his. The vibrator had slipped out and she was dripping from her fragrant pussy, the juices blended with the wine. "I think I love you, Master," she whispered, as their heartbeats blended slowly into one.

Marshall stiffened like he'd been struck by a dozen ceramic cats all at once. It was his worst fear come to life. The very attachment he'd never wanted from another living person, foisted on him once again. Not to mention how it proved that he'd just managed to completely brainwash her instead of setting her free as he'd intended.

"Meridian, listen to me," he said as kindly as possible. "You don't mean that. It's just the intensity of the domination experience talking."

"No," she lifted herself on tiptoes to kiss him. "It's my heart talking."

Wilder's cock found its way instinctively to her opening as they embraced. Their sexes pressed suggestively as he considered why he, too, seemed to get so worked up about their relationship. This was crazy and he knew it, but there was just no getting enough of this woman, at least not for tonight. Lifting her easily by the hips, he impaled her, sliding himself deep and satisfyingly into her warm, willing pussy.

The feel of her took his breath away. No woman had ever felt like this, no fuck had ever seemed so deep and...satisfying. Whoever this woman decided to spend her life with, would be the luckiest son of a bitch on the planet.

"Oh, yes, Master," she said, sighing and smiling in obvious relief as she wrapped her legs around his ass. "So good."

"This means nothing," he said, obligated to be the voice of reason, the proverbial wet blanket. "All this is...temporary."

"In that case," she buried her face against his neck. "May the slave beg to be fucked while she still is a slave? Please, Master?"

Wilder carried her to the brass bed, falling down on top of it with her. He was still inside her, still throbbing and aching. It was his plan to finish it—and her—off quick. Once freed of this erotic charge, they would both be able to think more clearly. But Meridian had no intention of letting him get off easily or half-heartedly.

"Want…need…restraint," she moaned, clutching at his shoulders with her small needy hands

"No, Meridian. We're done with BDSM and that's final."

"Master," she held out her crossed wrists. "Tie me…own me… I beg you."

He closed his eyes against the sight of her like this, but it burned into his brain. More than anything he wanted to honor this request, to show her what he could do, with his ropes, with his raw need to possess. But could he trust her with the results? More importantly, could he trust himself?

Questions surfaced suddenly now from deep in his mind, unanswered ones about his own past. Had the divorce all been Jenifer's fault, or had he done something to drive her away? Was there something in his possessiveness that was not positive and masterful but negative and stifling?

He couldn't take that chance. Which is why he needed this woman free of himself and all others like him.

"Master, restrain me," she repeated, her voice as fierce as it was female. "Tie my body."

It was as much a demand as anything else. Wilder felt the challenge rise in him all over again. Once more, he felt there was something to prove. "I'll tie you," he captured her wrists, pinning them overhead with a single hand. "But not with rope."

Meridian began to orgasm at once. "Oh, Master," she sighed. "This…is what…I need."

"You have no clue what you need," he slammed his cock in and out of her. "You are completely and utterly unaware of what is best for you."

"Oh, yes," she agreed enthusiastically, her breasts squashed against him, her back arched, her body coiled like a rope, wrapping about his, slender and sleek. "I yield...to you."

Again, his words had backfired. He was going to have to be the Dominant here, like it or not. She was throwing open her whole self and he would have to claim it, keep her from throwing herself into the void. "No more talking," he warned.

She restrained herself to whimpers and moans. Their flesh fused, easy and hot now, a liquid give and take that surpassed anything they'd had so far. It was a sacred moment, the only sound being their breathing, and the crackle of the fire. He could taste her surrender, its flavor far more intoxicating than the wine.

All the more reason to push this forward, to the conclusion, and then, as quickly as possible, drive back to the city and put this bizarre chapter in both their lives behind them.

Wilder's orgasm poured out of every nerve ending. It was like his whole body lighting up at once in one sheer, totally satisfying release, with his woman, his slave girl, crying out beneath him, completely had, possessed and used. Nothing could ever feel so good. On and on went his climax—the semen pouring out like it had been a week since his last orgasm and not a mere two hours.

She absorbed it all, exploding around him in a hundred meteor showers, each in turn urging him to harder and harder thrusts, the semen spurting from him like a fountain. When at last he'd regained his wits, he turned his attentions to the woman, the lady, the slave beneath him.

Meridian was still clutching sweetly, the way a woman should when treated right. It took her a while to come back down and he took his time, too, allowing his cock to recede naturally inside her. He felt so mellow that it seemed only natural to take just a little rest. A power nap before they hit the road back to the city. Couldn't do any harm. Besides things were so inviting, so peaceful in Meridian's arms. Like he really was home, just being with her.

Yes, he could spare a minute before ending this painful charade. Or maybe, he thought, as he rolled onto his back, he could take five or ten minutes. As if on cue, Meridian curled up under the crook of his arm, resting her head on his chest.

Five or ten minutes he repeated to himself, just before going down for the count.

Chapter Six

Merrie awoke with the sun shining on her face. She felt more refreshed and happier than she had in years. A bird was on the windowsill, chirping. Wilder was asleep beside her, on his back, breathing peacefully, his face bearing the most peaceful expression.

For some reason, instead of immediately reviewing the night's events in her mind, she went straight to the kitchen to prepare breakfast. There was time enough later for reason, recriminations and whatever else she would have to do to make sense of it all. For now, Merrie wanted only to enjoy.

Something had happened here, something between them, strong and real. Enough to silence, at least for a while, the doubts. She had told him she loved him, and while she was not ready to look at all the implications, or consider the long-term viability of that condition, it was still something that she could not ignore. He had moved her, claimed her and made a mark. To know what it meant they would have to play out this unique courtship.

Merrie retrieved the eggs from the small fridge and the butter and bacon, too. He had a cast iron skillet hanging on the wall, which she placed on the stove. Lastly, she pulled the loaf of bread down from the cupboard for toast.

How long had it been since she'd cooked breakfast for a man? When had a man last spent the entire night in her company, for that matter? Shaking back her unruly, tangled hair—she was so giddy, she didn't even care how it looked—she commenced frying the eggs.

It was only once the eggs began to spatter a bit that she remembered her nudity. Wilder had wanted her to cook like this last night. Was she being his little slave girl right now, then, or was this an act of free will on her part? She felt her throat. There was a collar in the bag of toys they'd bought and she had an irresistible urge to try it on. And why shouldn't she? This was supposed to be an experimental time, three days in which to try the lifestyle of Master and slave on for size.

Lord, but it had all happened so fast. In the space of a few short days, finding supposed online love with a nonexistent man, losing her job, and now gaining this strange new real-life relationship with her ex-boss. Her life was one big unanswered question all of a sudden. She'd pretty much disappeared off the radar as far as anyone was concerned. The only one who'd really worry about this was Kennedy. She made a mental note to call her later, at least let her know she was all right.

Standing on tiptoes, rubbing her tingling belly against the counter, Meridian found the plates. She took down two at first, but then she got this very warm and kinky idea not to give herself one. *Let him feed me again,* she thought, *if he's up for the challenge.*

Now she was whistling, another thing she hadn't done in ages. For some reason the man was bringing things out in her, all sorts of emotions, and not all bad. Yes, he was poison in the long run, but in this one tiny dose, how bad could it be? Anyway, he owed her and if she played her cards right, she might end up with the job she wanted from him after all.

That is if she could manage to make peace with herself, so she could ever be able to work with him again. That was part of what they were going to have to work out, and work through, in the next two days. The passion. The conflict. The sex.

Barely containing her strange excitement, she prepared him a heaping plate, along with a glass of orange juice and a mug of steaming coffee. As a finishing touch, she found the leather collar, cuffs and ankle straps. Her pulse raced as she put them on.

The collar was the most intriguing piece of all. Unlike the first time she'd modeled it, there was no mistaking its meaning in this new context. It was not jewelry, not decoration for a photo. It was utilitarian, for containment and control. There was even a ring on the front from which he'd attached the long chain he'd purchased. Her pussy melted as she fingered the innocent little strap at the end. It was a leash. With it, he could lead her…like some kind of treasured pet.

A little shiver went through her body as she let the chain rest between her breasts. Her nipples, she noticed, were still sensitive, and sore from the clamps. He'd done so much to her, would she ever be the same?

Merrie put the breakfast items on a tray, which she set down carefully on the nightstand. When everything was in place, she knelt beside the bed to wake him. He was on his stomach now, his face at the very edge of the mattress. She leaned forward, licking her lips.

It was the reverse of Cinderella, the captive girl kissing her domineering prince to life. He stirred slightly but did not yet awaken. She kissed him a second time, delighting in the feel of his strong, masculine lips. So full of power, and yet able to bestow such gentle loving.

A pleasant little chill went down her spine as she thought of him in these terms. Not just Master, but lover. Why did it matter so what he was to her, though? It was all just a game, wasn't it?

At last the blue eyes popped open and Merrie felt warmth pervade her flesh and fill her heart. Wilder was awake, and all seemed right with the world. "Good morning, my Master," she murmured in her best slave girl voice.

Wilder squinted, as if figuring something out. His brow furrowed and he sat up, like he'd been caught in the wrong bed with the wrong woman. "What the hell happened? Why are we still here?"

"You fell asleep, Master." She tried not to laugh at him. Why had she not seen what a teddy bear he was, cute, adorable, and almost comical underneath? "It's morning."

"The hell it is," he checked his Rolex, denying for the moment the evidence of his own eyes. "Blast it," he confirmed the hour. "I slept all night."

"That happens, Master, especially after good sex with your slave."

"What are you prattling about?" He eyed her. "I told you, we were done with that."

"But Master's slave has prepared breakfast," she indicated the tray. "Or would Master prefer first to make use of his slave?" She cupped her own breasts, holding them up to him.

"Don't play with me, Meridian. I'm not in the mood to be trifled with."

Merrie scooted back and put her head to the floor. "The slave begs punishment for offending Master."

Her heart was thundering in her chest. Was she really trifling with him or not? She wasn't sure. It had started lighthearted enough, but there was no telling where it could go with a man like this. And she was not altogether sure she was not provoking him at some level, just to get a response.

"Get up, Meridian," said Wilder. "And listen carefully."

She rose to her feet, warily.

"Whatever you think you are doing, it doesn't work that way," he said.

"I don't understand, Master."

"Slaves don't control their own experiences, not even the seemingly negative ones. As much as you think you are being obedient, you are just following your own will, doing just what you like. You still haven't learned your lesson, have you? You still think there is something noble and romantic about being an owned woman."

She bit her lip. "No," she replied quickly and defiantly before she could come to her senses. "I have not learned my lesson. I'm a bad slave…Master."

Marshall's face lit with a new clarity, a new purpose, as if he were born to do this one thing, to control and possess her. What was the old saying, she thought grimly, be careful what you wish for, you might get it?

"Very well, you had your chance to end this. I will continue dominating you, Meridian. But you will find it's not so pleasant, this ever escalating loss of control you insist on experiencing."

"I am ready to be punished," she stood proudly, her buttocks already clenching in anticipation of the flogger. "For any actions that have displeased you."

"No," he shook his head. "You are not ready. Go and stand in that corner. Face the wall until I tell you to come out."

Meridian blinked. She'd wanted to be thrown to the floor, flogged and ravished, not treated as a small child.

"And you will take off the collar and cuffs," he added. "You wear them by my command only."

"Yes," she pouted. "Master."

Merrie removed the leather restraints, put them on the nightstand and went to the corner of the room.

"Arms at your side, back straight," he called.

She obeyed, tensing her body like a soldier's. Her eyes glared at the sharply intersecting rows of wooden logs. It was a corner, all right, and she was a punished woman, standing in it.

Wilder took his time eating the breakfast she'd prepared. "I like my eggs over easy," he informed her, as if she had any intention of doing this for him ever again.

Merrie clenched her teeth. This was not at all fun, not at all sexy.

"Toast is a little burnt, too."

She wanted to tell him off, but that would probably just add to his satisfaction. "So sorry," she dripped sarcastically. "Master."

He continued his chewing, alternating with sips of the coffee. Surely he would save her something?

"Do you know what my nickname was for Jenifer? My ex-wife?" He asked, the sudden shift in the conversation catching her off-guard.

"TB. I called her TB. Short for Treacherous Bitch. She claimed to be submissive, too. Wanted to be a slave more than anything in the world. In reality, though, there's only one thing keeps a female subservient. And that's fear. Unless she's just playing a man for his money. Don't get me wrong, I don't blame your gender. You tend to be physically weaker, you have fewer opportunities, and so you do what you must to survive. I know Jenifer had her problems, a rough childhood. She was a masochist in some ways, in other ways just a mixed-up kid. Bottom line, I can't fault her for being a woman."

"How generous of you," Merrie couldn't resist commenting.

"See?" He laughed. "I've already provoked you out of your slave act. It's only fear keeping you in check. If you thought you could get away with it, you would come at me claws flying, right this second."

Her lips trembled. "Maybe it's not me who's so afraid. Did you stop to think of that?"

Wilder cursed under his breath. "Go and fetch the paddle from the bag. The big one."

It was long and made of polished wood. She retrieved it and handed it to him, avoiding eye contact.

He tested it out in the air right in front of her. "Sure you don't want to go home and call it a day yet...Miss Hunter?"

She turned up her nose very slightly. "No, Master."

He shook his head. "You're a stubborn one. I can see I'll have to turn up the heat on you."

She licked her lips. She was feeling plenty of heat already, thank you very much.

He made her lie across the wooden table, her soft breasts pressed to the hard, unyielding surface, the wood prickling her skin. Then he had her put her hands palm down, stretched above her head. Losing her right to control her own motions made her a little skittish, as did not being able to see what he was going to do behind her. It was going to sting, she knew that, and it could also be sexual, that much was clear.

The anticipation was excruciating, causing her to clench her buttocks as she felt the liquid collecting at the opening to her pussy.

Resting his hand lightly on her back, he said, "This is a more advanced lesson. If at any point it is too much to handle, use the word Rumplestiltskin, and whatever is happening will end immediately. If you do choose to invoke the safe word, however, know that I will take you home, on the spot, no ifs, ands or buts."

"Yes, Master."

She'd heard of safe words. They were used to keep submissives from being accidentally injured. She wasn't sure whether this made her feel better or worse. Certainly having her ass out like this, exposed, unable to see what he might do was invoking things in her, bringing her to new levels of alertness and readiness.

There was fear, too, and yearning, and wonder. And need—for this man, for all the things he could give her and all the things he could make her feel.

"And you will also give me your word at that point never to try and live out these fantasies again."

Merrie did not understand this at all. What did he want from her? Why was he being so cruel? He knew she craved this, craved him. Yet it was not her place to object or understand. "I agree to your terms," she whispered. "Master."

Wilder touched the paddle to her ass. "You may cry out, scream and beg in any way," he let her know. "But I will not relent unless you say the word."

"Yes, Master." Merrie whimpered at the touch of it, hard and heavy, promising mayhem. Her every nerve fiber was already crying out.

He left her a moment, going to the kitchen. Oh, god, what was he getting? Something to use on her, she feared. Straining desperately, she tried to hear, tried to get some heads-up on what might be coming. It was so tempting to get up and run. Or else to lie here and cry, the tears dripping from her cheek onto the wooden table.

Talk about humiliation—spread like this on a piece of furniture. She could only imagine if anyone saw her like this, anyone she knew. What would they do or say? She wondered. What would they think?

Merrie tensed. He was coming back. Chills ran up and down her spine. Was he holding anything? She dreaded his coming, and yet the time without him had felt like forever. She'd never needed a man before, never felt so dependent, and yet so deliciously free in the process. Free to be herself. To be the female she yearned to be in her heart.

"Knowing she can be punished by her owner," he returned to caress her once again, "is the slave's key to true yielding. It makes her wet and ready at all times. She is subject, in a way no standard mate could ever be."

Merrie moaned as he ran his finger over the crack of her pussy, already dripping wet. The touch was a light kiss to her inner lips, but also an electric zap, sending spasms to her core.

Abruptly, he pulled the finger away and struck her with the paddle. It was a strict, humiliating blow. Before she could fully register the heat of it, he was back to her pussy. This time pushing between the swollen, eager lips.

"Hold still," he chastened as he found her clit.

Merrie tried to obey, but failed. Her own senses were betraying her. The man was taking over her body, with his teasing, his invasion, his total domination of her being.

Wilder sought to focus her with another blow of the paddle.

"I am going to take you anally," he informed her, his finger tracing a line up and down her bowed spine. "But not 'til you beg me."

"Yes," she groaned, her belly burning as hot as her buttocks. "Oh, yes, Master."

He slid his fingers deeper into her sex, which offered him no opposition. "Do not presume to agree too readily. You have no idea the submission that will be required of you first."

Merrie contemplated the ominous words, even as he paddled her again, making her stinging ass cheeks quiver like jelly. She was losing her bearing now, not sure what to wish for, whether more of this…or sex…or nothing

"You may thank me for disciplining you."

"Thank you, Master," said she, breathless.

"Thank you for paddling my naughty little slave ass, Master,'" he coached.

Meridian repeated the phrase, hot, degrading and sexy. She was his, to deal with as he saw fit. This made him happy and hard and it was foreplay. Advance preparation for the inevitable invasion of her ass.

"There will be no more mercy for you," he informed her. "Every hour you don't throw in the towel, I'll only push you harder."

"Truly, Master?"

"I have to do this," he reminded. "For your own good. To cure you."

He was being true to the rules of their encounter, but part of her wanted this to mean something more, something intimate, as befitting a man and a woman…a couple…that had shared in so much already.

"Fuck my fingers, slave girl, and let's wipe those foolish stars out of your eyes, once and for all."

Merrie raised her hips, pushing herself at him, shamelessly. Her body was confused, as was her heart.

"Come for me, slave girl. You have 'til the count of ten."

She gritted her teeth. Was he kidding?

"One. Two. Three."

Merrie grunted, trying to increase the friction. She was covered in sweat now, her breasts squashed, her thighs and ass totally exposed. He was only up to number six and she'd never been more horny or more desperate in her life.

"Seven. Eight. Nine."

"Oh, Master," she moaned. "Need…more…time."

"Ten," he called, and the climax arrived, but it was too late.

"Oh, Master, please, give me another chance."

She felt something cold on the back of her thigh. "No," he said, sliding the ice cube up to her hips. "You had one chance and you blew it."

Meridian writhed, the sheer contrast of the frozen liquid on the heat of her punished behind playing havoc with her senses. "Master…I'm sorry…I failed."

"I don't doubt that you are," he circled the ice around her pussy. "But has it occurred to you I wanted you to fail? It is a common technique among Masters. To make the slave girl even more helpless and dependent."

"Y-Yes, Master."

"I want you to relax your muscles." The ice was directly over her crack, the melting substance mixing with her own more viscous fluids. "I want you to take this inside you. All the way."

"Master?"

He couldn't possibly put the ice…in there, could he?

Was this her punishment then, or just part of his overall entertainment plan?

The cube parted her lips, slowly, but relentlessly. The sensation was bitter cold, but also like a blazing heat.

"Fuck the ice cube, slave girl," her Master encouraged. "Don't think, just do."

Merrie complied, lifting, writhing and otherwise making a complete and total wench out of herself.

"Enough." He slid the ice out, up her crack and onto her lower back. He left it there to melt.

"No one has ever given me as much grief as you have," he placed his palm over her ass. "Least of all a woman."

Merrie tried to hide her pride at the distinction. "Really, Master?"

He smacked her with the flesh of his hand. It was a smooth, expert blow, designed to put a woman safely and quickly in her place. "You know very well what I'm saying. Don't even pretend to be surprised."

She bit her lip. "No, Master."

This, she decided, would be a very poor time to laugh.

"One would almost think you were asking for it," he mused.

"Never, Master."

He spanked her again, making her tailbone wiggle. "You are a splendid piece of ass, Merrie. You don't mind if I call you that, do you?"

Merrie couldn't resist the chance to play with him a little. "Which, Master? Merrie or piece of ass? Either is fine…depending on the context."

Wilder lifted something off the table. A jar of some kind, which he was opening. "I forget what I'm dealing with in you, sometimes," he conceded. "Tell me, this, though. Do you think your dreams and fantasies about me have any place in the real world?"

"What fantasies?" She tensed. The cream was cold and slippery and wet.

He shifted the position of his fingers so he was inside her ass and pussy both, pushing, challenging. "The ones you have about me at staff meetings. And don't think I didn't notice. I know when women want me."

She shifted a little on her bare toes. The smug bastard. He probably really did know—that was the hell of it. What chance did any woman stand? Especially one with her wild imagination and thin skin?

This is only an experiment. Just a game. I can make it through.

She said the words over and over, even as the confession poured from her mouth. "I saw you as a pirate," she breathed. "You had just kidnapped me to be your slave."

"Ah, yes. All quite romantic, isn't it?" He patted her ass, then spanked her, just because he could. "Too bad reality never lives up to the dreams we have."

Merrie jumped at his touch, her belly pressing even harder against the wood. She couldn't focus on conversation. She needed attention. She needed handling. Didn't he see what he'd done to her? He'd changed her, made her crave his touch.

"Master," she squirmed. "Oh, Master…I need to come."

Immediately, he removed his finger to the edge of her pussy to deny her. *Should have kept my mouth shut,* she chided herself.

"Master knows what you need. You are a prideful slave girl. You need to be taught your lesson."

She flooded at the notion of such intimate control. "If I were really owned," she panted. "Truly owned, what would happen to me?"

"New slave girls are often kept in cages," he fed her prurient interest. "They are taken out only to be exercised and fucked."

"B-But how do they eat?"

He smacked her ass. "You're the one with all the fantasies, tell me."

Merrie sighed hotly, her sex clenching, her scent filling the air. "Would she take scraps…from Master's hand?"

He flicked her clitoris, bringing her savagely to the brink. "Yes. Or from a dish. A slave girl can be made to eat from a dish on the floor."

"Oh...Master..." Her legs were shaking. It was like an electric surge, making her muscles and nerves respond of their own accord.

"Whose body is this?" he inquired.

"Yours, Master."

"Whose pussy?"

"Oh..." The words wouldn't form.

"Whose ass?"

She screamed as he pinched her, but it didn't hurt, not like regular pain. It was more like the crop or the clamps, better still.

"I can deny you my touch, you know. That's the worst punishment, do you realize that?"

"Don't," she thrashed her head. "Don't...please."

"I warned you, this wasn't a game."

"Master," she cried into the sudden emptiness. "My Master...please."

He left her momentarily in the void. An anti-orgasm, sheer conquest by feelings of total deprivation, her body turning in upon itself. She was unable to move, but if she could, there was nothing in the universe she would have sought but him. His touch. His domination. Oh, how he had her now, spread before him, her mind and body, opened, completely on display.

For the first time she had an inkling of real slavery. "Please, Master. Fuck me, beat me...anything."

"You remember what I told you earlier? What you would have to do?" he prodded.

Her first ass fucking! He'd told her earlier how he would make her beg for it when the time was right—surely this was it.

"Yes," she moaned. "Oh, Master, fuck your slave's ass."

He applied more of the cream, lubricating her even deeper. "Whose ass is this?"

"Yours, Master. Fuck it. Fuck it hard."

"I intend to, slave girl." The end of his cock pressed against her tight opening. She cried out, as though he were already inside her.

"M...aster..."

"Concentrate on your breathing," he slid the first inch home. "We have a long way to go."

But where was it they were going exactly? And what did she feel for him, really? Would she have come this far, taken this many risks if it was only a game, an exercise in lust? What did it mean that she had learned to catalogue his moods, and that she lost herself so completely at the sight of him, even when he was at his worst? For that matter, what had compelled him to ask her here to this cabin, to enter this arrangement—really?

"So...I've been thinking. How would you like to replace Sharon? I've seen the way you look at her, green with envy. Tell me the thought's never crossed your mind, being my little helper?" he teased. "I'm sure we could put you to work. Dress you in nice short skirts." In went his cock, a little further. "Have you fetch coffee at the meetings like a good little slave-secretary."

Merrie groaned as Marshall conquered her, with his words and his dick.

The thought of becoming like Sharon scandalized her, but also made her horny as hell. Prancing around the office in tight clothes, running servile errands, batting her eyelashes, begging with her eyes to be stripped and used for the boss' amusement. Gritting her teeth, she did her best to block it out as she worked on accommodating the man's shaft. Which at the moment was the center of her world, just as he'd said it would be.

I'm being fucked in my ass, she thought, *filled by the cock and will of a man.* She pictured his shaft, the pulsing veins, the thick base, the sloping tip. She was glad to have it in this new way—a little terrified, but also quite thoroughly intoxicated.

"You could serve coffee and pastry on your knees to the men," he pressed on. "When we hold our meetings. Maybe relieve their pressure a little with that mouth of yours."

"Yes, Master..." Her voice was soft and high, weak and agonizingly female as he made her take another inch, and then another. She was nothing but an open crater of need now, nothing but a surrendered vessel.

"What do you want?" he queried.

She knew the answer, or thought she did. "I want...to be used...taken by you."

"No," he grasped her hips, creating yet another form of pressure, maddeningly delicious. "You are not to want anything. If Master uses you or does not use you, that is Master's business and not your own. You keep thinking you are allowed to have a will as a slave. But you are not. Ever."

"Master, forgive me." Her pussy was dripping, signaling her soft availability, her literal, physical need to appease. If only she could touch herself, just for a moment.

Wilder moved his cock in and out, testing the already conquered ground. "A Master would give this to anyone," he explained, referring to her own well-stuffed channel. "He would no more balk at loaning your ass, pussy or mouth than he would at giving out a CD or a power drill. And he would make sure you knew that, every minute of your life."

"I'd be property," moaned Merrie, pushing herself against him, wanting more, wanting him to the hilt if she could stand it without splitting wide open. "My body…owned… Oh, Master, please, tell me more."

"A slave knows fear, insecurity. Walks a fine line."

"But…she also…feels…everything," she panted in counterpoint.

Wilder pulled his penis out of her abruptly, cutting short her mounting pleasure. Was there no end to this man's ability to tease?

"You're wrong. You think you know," he took her by the hair, just hard enough to control her and secure her attention. "But you don't. You think you can anticipate. You can't."

He pushed her to her knees on the floor—she could hardly have stood upright had he released her.

"Put your hand in your pussy. Nice and deep."

She looked up at him in shock and wonder. He really was in control. Really was the Master.

"Play with yourself," he encouraged, his voice promising yet another world of delight. "Play with your pussy for your Master."

Merrie flushed red, feeling like a naughty teenager and a whore rolled into one.

"That's it," he encouraged with all the confidence in the world. "Surrender, don't fight it. Take it to a new level. Do it, as my slave and mine alone."

She rocked against her fingers. She liked this kind of talk very much.

"Come for me, yes, come for your Master."

His words, the sudden power of the command tripped off just the right trigger. It was like reflex pleasure, waves ripping through her, and with them endless spasms of white-hot satisfaction. A primal release, not of her making, not like masturbating at all. She grunted low, looking up at him for approval, a sleek little thing at his feet, a female animal, orgasming on command, performing while he watched, his eyes engaging, promising.

The sensations, the feeling of the floor pressing her kneecaps, the smell of sweet pine and even sweeter sex and the sound of Master's contented breathing, all of them together, wrapping around her, lifting her up an enormous rollercoaster and then back down. Once, twice, three times.

"Mmm," she sighed, smiling up at him when she'd finally come down from the clouds.

He gave her no time to recover. "I need you to hold up your breasts, open your mouth and look at me. Come now, don't keep Master waiting. That's a good slave."

She did as she was told, feeling awkward, but oddly sexy, and nasty at the same time.

"A Master can degrade you," he stroked himself. "Any way he likes. But he must also respect and honor the gift of your submission."

The sight of Marshall's cock had her mesmerized. He handled it just so, long manly pulls up and down the length of it. He'd used a washcloth to clean himself, and now it looked brand spanking new, firm and proud and ready. Its eye looking straight at her.

Merrie held her position, awaiting the inevitable. His face reddened, features tightening in a beautiful expression, every detail of which she wanted to memorize. He was going to come. On her.

One final grunt, a last squeeze and his semen was shooting directly at her. The first blast landed on her delicately extended tongue. He hit her cheeks next, then the tip of her nose and finally a nice healthy spray across her breasts. She relished the man's come, this visible sign indicating that he was indeed happy with her, pleased with his temporary slave.

It was an experience she would never have enjoyed in any other role. The act itself, performed by a lesser man could have been totally demeaning, and yet from him—her temporary Master—it was elevated into the category of a gift. A sacred offering made to her tingling, owned flesh.

He continued milking himself, giving her every drop. Then he had her suck him clean. At last he told her to put her hands in front of her, wrists crossed.

"My semen marks you," he told her, binding her with the long piece of rope he took off the table. "It is removed only by my hand."

She sighed, feeling so sweet and soft as he took a cloth and cleaned her face and breasts, thoroughly, delicately. A moment later they were walking out the cabin door into the sunshine, not a clue on her part where they were going.

It's really true, she smiled to herself, the full reality hitting home. *I'm a slave today. A slave today,* she repeated the words. *A slave today.*

But what about tomorrow and the next day and the next? That was the real question. Did this experiment have legs? Would they have anything to do with each other when it was all said and done? She had told him she loved him. He'd said it was just a reaction to what he was doing to her and she'd taken his word for it. Still, there were things to think about. Things to consider. The underlying bonds, the strange reactions they engendered in one another. The way she leaped at his touch and came for him. The way she had come to trust him with her body and her dreams. The way she worried so for his intensity, and what it might be doing to him inside. The way she saw him when she closed her eyes, and felt so fiercely competitive with him for no apparent reason. And the way she did not want these three days to ever end. For the first time since her arrival, she started praying for the time to slow down, so she somehow had time to understand it all. Before it was too late. And he was gone from her life.

*****

Wilder stood guard over the beautiful woman washing herself in the creek. Strange how he had never before stopped to appreciate just how breathtaking Meridian was. She was always pretty to him, yes, but never before had he noticed this…radiance. Was it new in her or had he simply grown more observant?

She seemed lost in her own private world, running her bound hands over her body, sluicing the clear water down her delicious pale curves with the rough, brown sponge he'd provided. One leg extended, in an unconscious gesture of self-offering. The knee-deep water was cold and at first she had balked. Then he'd told her it was the lot of slaves to bathe where they were told. Her green eyes lit and suddenly she was his accomplice, as always effecting her own enslavement with her sensual enthusiasm.

It was this way with intelligent, submissive women. They did the work of subjugation largely by themselves. Meridian was the smartest he'd ever seen. And the most intoxicating. How could he look upon her and not want to cherish, possess and own her? How could his heart not grow warm and his cock grow hard?

Was this love? He'd given up understanding his own feelings anymore, if indeed he ever had. Too many times they had led him into betrayal and false hope. She was simply a gorgeous female, the kind to catch any man's eye and he was responding like any other male.

Generic, that's what it was. And situational. The result of the intense passions of Dominance and submission, released along strange emotional channels. He'd seen it in her, this false glow of love, and now he was seeing it in himself. Just the splendor of possession. It would all fade when they left. It would have to, so she could be free to go after the life she wanted and needed when they got back home. A life free of him and his sexual demands.

Both her nipples peaked prominently, now, hardened to bullets at the center of her proud upturned breasts. Her hair hung wet about her shoulders, giving her the look of a fire-haired sprite, sunlight glinting off the rich copper. She had never looked so magnificent in the office, in her conservative skirt suits and starched blouses, or even in her red dress at the hotel. Distracting, yes, but never so entirely…female.

She was all woman in this place, out in the open, in the primeval forest, under his complete protection, complete control. For all she knew some bear could tear out of the woods or a wildcat rip her to shreds. Yet here she was, in sensuous slow motion, cleaning her body as though she were in the most peaceful of gardens.

Emotions tore at his gut—the work of invisible wildcats and bears, a half dozen at least. Extreme responsibility, bordering on guilt, foremost among them. He oughtn't to be putting her through this. It had taken months to work Jenifer up to this level of intensity in her slavery. Only with very experienced submissives could a man expect to exercise this kind of dominance. It was true, Meridian had teased him and begged for him to take more from her, especially this morning, but he couldn't blame her for that. It was up to him to keep the situation in check and to know her limits, even if she did not.

Clearly, this was no ordinary woman. She had the ability to get under his skin. To keep him off-balance. And it wasn't only her beauty, it was her mind, her damnable spirit. And her heart. He'd never seen a heart like that in a female. Except his mother, whose endurance in the midst of a family of monsters ought to have put her up for the Congressional Medal of Honor.

It was a powerful, powerful thing to have a woman like Meridian Hunter tethered, naked and humbled, dependent upon him for her very existence. His cock raged at the thought. His blood pounded. He'd never known such total, unabashed pleasure.

And looking at her now, at her erotic ablutions, he had a sneaking suspicion that she was experiencing the flipside. The glow of submission. The complete peace and release that comes from being under another's mastery. It was called subspace by some—the mental place the submissive enters in her surrender. For others it was a kind of spiraling down into a place of openness, oneness with something bigger in creation.

In such a mode, one did not notice one's nudity per se, or the coldness of the water. Nor did one worry what the Master would do next, though the vague anticipation, the unknown element of it all, was definitely part of the thrill.

Wilder ran through the options in his mind of how to play with his slave on this fine day in the mountains. Tease her, of course, and bring her to new levels of degradation. She must...love it, but also hate it. She must feel good, but in the end, she must above all, come away wanting never, ever to do this sort of thing again.

In short, she must experience a complete and total contradiction.

He rubbed the back of his neck. *Just what have I gotten myself into*? He pondered that question for the millionth time in the last twenty-four hours.

*****

Meridian walked through the high grass, her wrist firmly leashed. She was blindfolded and naked, being led by her Master. He had his riding crop with him, and when necessary, he would reach around and flick her with the end of it, just to remind her to keep the pace.

She was on fire with sexual need. Her thighs were slick and as she moved, she could feel the friction, the liquid heat. Every blade of the waist-high grass was itself like a whip on her skin. Her breasts were swollen, and so sensitive that with each little brush of a bug or gust of wind she felt spasms all the way down to her pussy.

There was no mistaking how it all turned her on, no disguising the effects of her Master's newest level of domination. It wasn't just being led through the meadow like this, but the inherent trust, the passionate surrender required. She could not see. She was as helpless as a woman could be. She was…owned.

Where were they going? And what would he do when they got there? She prayed it would be sex. Any kind of sex. He hadn't explicitly forbidden her from speaking, but somehow, it did not feel appropriate under the circumstances.

Merrie continued forward, following the tug of the leash, keeping it from growing too taut, and always—always—following his sweet, familiar scent. At one point an insect landed on her ass, and she tried to wriggle it away. Master snapped the crop down on her buttock, whether to keep her from moving like that or to remove the fly, she wasn't sure. Either way, the sensation sent ripples down her spine.

"Come, slave," he tugged at the light chain attached to her collar.

Merrie clenched her pussy muscles. He was her Master. She had to obey him. No matter what.

"Stop," he said at last. "Good girl."

She lifted her head as he nuzzled her cheek with his hand. She was so fucking horny. If only she could see him, if only she was free. But her world was warm and dark, filled with buzzing and brushing and warm sunshine and rustling grass and underneath the soles of her feet, the dirt, cool and energized and almost living in its fecundity. And Him. Master. The center of it all.

"Is this what you want?" He guided her down to her knees, her head to the crotch of his khakis. She found the zipper already open, the hard shaft poking through.

She fell on Marshall Wilder's dick, wanting to devour it whole.

"Earn it," he took her by the hair, holding her at bay.

Marshall put her on all fours while he played with her body using the crop, up and down her back, the light touches sizzling like a bullwhip. Next he reached down with the vibrator—god, she didn't even know he'd brought it along—and shoved it into place, turning her insides to mush.

But the cruelest instrument of all was his voice.

"Do you know, Meridian, the number of women I have had to counsel, cure and heal over the years as a result of abusive Master/slave relationships?"

She shook her head, sweat forming, even as her teeth chattered in the sunshine.

"So far I've held back the worst stories of what can happen, in order to spare you. Maybe that was weakness on my part. The truth is, you are too stubborn for your own good. The world is about power, Meridian. To survive, you have to have enough of it to fight off everyone else. And god help anyone who gives their power away to another, especially under the guise of playing Master and slave. Have you ever heard of the Talis stories?"

Merrie was beyond speech. An orgasm was gripping her already. But what was he doing? Something was pushing at her from behind. Something intended for her ass. Oh, god, it was the butt plug. Instinctively she clamped tight, forcing him to interrupt his train of thought.

"You need to relax your muscles," he chided, smacking her as though she were being willfully disobedient. "Or else you will find yourself crawling back to the cabin on your hands and knees for a whipping."

She whimpered as he pushed the plug into place. Did her feelings, her preferences mean nothing? Did it not matter one little bit that she was out of her mind wanting him inside her right now? She couldn't care less for either his lectures or his butt plugs.

But that was the point, wasn't it? The secret turn-on of slavery. Being totally free because the man made all the choices. Knowing you need never fear if you were pleasing because the man would use you exactly as he wanted, as his total object of pleasure.

Her pussy gushed as the pressure mounted. She was full, and possessed. Out in the open, completely helpless.

"The Talis books are a series of fantasy books outlining a world in which women are slaves, owned by men. It's a primitive, brutal world, but for various reasons, the books have a cult following in ours. People live them out, online and in real life. They have their own Talis communities and in them the females are property, for real. They sleep with all the males as ordered, they are beaten, confined, and they may even be sold. We have words for these activities in our language. Abuse. Assault. Kidnapping."

She pushed her ass against the plug, willing it to be a cock. Her sex cried out silently, so close to completion, and yet hanging, in the middle of space, a trigger-pull away from climax.

"Must…come…Master."

"I ought to just take full-time possession of you flat out," he said. "Just to keep you safe from all that."

Merrie collapsed to her belly, caught in the throes of her passion. God, how she wished he would. "Oh, Master."

"Turn over," he commanded, ordering her to her back. He pulled out the vibrator, and mounted her swiftly, imperiously. The plug pushed in from below like a second lover, sandwiched underneath her. Merrie was completely splayed open. Everything but the sensations forgotten. Grunting, he rolled her over. She cried out, as they exploded together, clinging—no order, no hierarchy, just a jumbled coupling, slithering and seething in the grass. Two bodies, fit and strong, seeking something in flesh that their hearts and minds could not yet accept.

"Master," she whispered when the fever had subsided. "I feel it again… I…I love you."

Wilder's reaction was swift and fierce. "Damn it," he cried. "Damn it all to hell. I thought we talked about this. I thought it settled."

She was up off the ground and over his shoulder in an instant, his hand on her ass, balancing her like a sack of potatoes.

"Put me down," she cried, forgetting the Master part.

He made no response. Taking her back across the field, he stormed inside the cabin and tossed her down onto the bed. "Get dressed," he said, his voice cold and distant.

"But why? Our time's not up." She'd never seen him like this, face expressionless, his eyes so distant.

"Because the fun and games are finished Meridian. This little experiment is over. You're going home now, end of story."

She felt indignation rising, too little, too late to cover the deep wave of rejection she already felt. "That's it, then?" she asked, injecting the query with as much disdain as possible. "No explanations? No lectures? No famous Wilder debriefing first?"

"That's not going to happen. Nothing between us is going to happen. Ever again." It was like everything human in him had died back there in that field.

She blinked back the tears, snatching up her underwear. "Fine," she spat, though she was anything but. "Anyway, I don't really love you, do I? It's just a 'reaction'. It'll pass as soon as we get out of here, don't worry."

He was watching her like a hawk and it was too much to endure. "I'll thank you to give me some privacy."

His lips twinged, for just a moment, like he wanted to say something else. "I'll be in the car. Come out when you're ready."

"Go to hell," she spat.

A few minutes later she came out, and got into the Porsche, slamming the door.

"Put on your seatbelt," he told her.

She glared, eyes like lasers. "I'm not your slave anymore, remember?"

"Do it as my employee, then," he put the car in reverse, backing down the path from the house. "Consider it a direct order."

She snorted with as much venom as she could manage. "You must have a memory problem, Wilder, I quit, remember?"

"And I have chosen not to accept your resignation. Instead, I'm promoting you."

"I don't want the job. I'd rather sweep floors at a Quick Burger."

"What if I doubled my previous offer? And promised you development opportunities in Wilder Industries as a whole."

Merrie tried to keep her tone neutral, though her pulse raced at the possibilities. "You're insane, Wilder, we couldn't even be in the same room, let alone work together."

"It's your choice," he shrugged. "Although I'm a bit disappointed."

The words struck her like a knife to her gut, thought she wasn't sure why she should possibly care what opinion he had of her. "What makes you say that?"

"I'd thought you were made of stronger stuff."

They were silent for a while. Her head began to pound. This was all too much, way too fast. A few weeks ago, she'd been a happy, lonely single woman with a nice safe career path. Now she was an ex-sex slave contemplating the career offer of a lifetime, all the while deciding which she wanted to do more—scratch this man's eyes out or bury her head in his chest and cry until he made everything all right again.

"I can take it if you can," she said at last.

"You'll start Monday," he replied, not taking his eyes off the road. "We'll get you up and running, see how it develops. Agreed?"

"Agreed," she replied, though she had absolutely, positively no idea how she was going to handle this, or him.

Mentally counting the days until Monday, she tried to see how far away she could get. Was Antarctica out of the question?

Chapter Seven

Kennedy sat on the edge of Meridian's desk, her already large eyes wide as moons. "Wow, that is one hot story," she said huskily, having finally badgered her boss into sharing the full account of the ill-fated trip to the cabin.

Merrie frowned from the couch. As usual the young woman was seeing only the light part, the sexy part. It was her age, of course. Wait until life kicked her around some, then she'd see what it was really all about. Pain. Disappointment. Loss.

"Maybe for a confessions magazine, Kennedy, but not for the real world. He hurt me. Hell, we hurt each other. It was a terrible mismatch and we barely survived the ordeal."

Kennedy flicked her toes thoughtfully, bobbing her lightweight sandal off the end of the biggest one. It was, Meridian knew, one of the many postures the young woman affected when she was going to try and make trouble. Sure enough, she said, "But look at the job he gave you. How can you complain about that?"

"He's buying me off, Kennedy. Don't you understand?"

Kennedy wrinkled her nose. "Yes, I do. What I don't see is how it's a bad thing. He has more money than he knows what to do with. Why not let him share some with you?"

Merrie lay her head back on the leather. Soon she would be putting this couch in her new office, the one Wilder was still occupying until his expected departure. She was to take over at that point, if she survived. He'd been hell to work for since they'd gotten back, managing to stay on her case almost constantly. It was all she could do not to tell him where to get off and quit all over again.

"Miss Hunter. Are you there?" The buzzing intercom nearly caused her to burst out of her skin. It had been a good fifteen minutes since she'd heard it and she was hoping against all hope that he'd actually decided to give his finger—and her—a rest. "I want those projections for fourth quarter," said Wilder. "And a cup of coffee. Real creamer, no more of that powdered garbage."

"You see," Merrie waved to the infernal speaker box. "This is what I have to put up with. Only four days back, and I'm ready to go out of my mind. He knows it's not my job to get him coffee. So why does he ask?"

"Admittedly that does suck," said the young woman whose ensemble for the day consisted of lime green pants painted over long legs and a pink tank top. "But he is leaving," she reminded. "And then you can do what you like."

"Right, like he won't be able to call or fax me constantly."

"And he will," she acknowledged. "If you don't draw the line with him."

Meridian tried to come up with a snappy retort but couldn't. She continued to think about it all the way down to the CEO's office. *Kennedy is right,* she decided. *I don't have to put up with this. There are limits.*

And I will tell him that, too, she thought to herself as she rummaged in the break room fridge for some real creamer for his coffee. The question being, when would she, and what was holding her back? It wasn't like she enjoyed this treatment or anything. They'd played their dominant sex games, and they'd moved on. It was supposed to be all business now. A fact he had managed so far to reinforce by taking every opportunity to treat her with an almost inhuman disdain.

Marching into his office, straight past Sharon, who was sitting at her desk staring daggers, Merrie placed the perfect cup of coffee on his desk. "This can't continue," she announced.

Wilder ignored her. "I've been going over the spreadsheets again. Do you realize the dip in profit to loss ratio we've suffered in our Far Eastern money market accounts?"

"Are you listening to a word I'm saying?" she demanded.

He continued to grumble over the numbers on his monitor. Just four days into this new job, and he was already involving her in half his empire. Reaching for his coffee, he took a sip. "Needs sugar," he said.

She tried to keep her cool. "I thought you didn't like sugar."

"In the morning, no. By afternoon, yes. Must I explain everything to you, Miss Hunter?"

Merrie held her tongue. Taking the cup, a pleasant smile plastered on her face, she said. "My bad, sir, let me fix it at once."

She'd fix it all right, with a nice dose of salt.

Maybe that would give him a little taste of his own medicine. Enough was enough. It was bad enough he ruled her nights, making her toss and turn and burn, sweat-soaked in her sheets, yearning for his touch, his masterful commands that would make her, force her to feel all the wicked female things inside her.

It was supposed to have been an experiment at the cabin, a lesson to cure her, but somehow it had only whetted her appetite for more. How could another man ever do those things to her? How could she ever give herself like that again? He'd taken everything. Used and exploited her, but also lifted her to heights of ecstasy. As his slave she'd known more bliss, more reverence than she'd ever felt as anyone's date or girlfriend.

Masturbating did no good whatsoever. Repeatedly, she'd humped her bed, stuffed herself with her vibrator on high, covering her face with the pillow to muffle the screams. She'd even tied herself so she could feel the constriction and the restraint, but that only made her hornier and emptier inside. Just this morning she'd gone into the ladies' room to take her hand to her own ass, clawing at her panties so she could spank her bare buttocks to the point of tears.

She was confused and hot and...lost. And it was this man's fault. Not that he cared. Not that he gave anything close to a damn about her feelings. All that talk about being a Master and keeping by her side was all an act after all. In the end, he was nothing but a mean chauvinist...prick.

Smiling with the first satisfaction she'd felt in days, she upended the saltshaker. When it came out too slowly, she unscrewed the top and poured the contents in directly.

The white crystals disappeared to the bottom. She stirred them in with a nearby spoon.

Merrie couldn't wait to see the look on his face. It would be such a beautiful comeuppance. Then again, what if it made him angry? What if he decided to…punish her?

Merrie licked her lips. Was that what she wanted? To get him to act like her Master again? Taking a deep breath, she took the cup and began her journey back to chauvinist pig central. Time to see what the man is made of, she thought somberly.

* * * * *

Marshall Wilder pushed his erection down in his trousers. Every encounter with Meridian was worse than the last. If he could be sure how long she was going to take getting him his coffee, he could masturbate while she was gone. But that would leave the mental problem. He'd tried affecting every emotion towards her from condescension to pure contempt to get her out of his mind, but so far nothing worked.

His latest hope was that Meridian might quit out of sheer exasperation at having to take over some of Sharon's minor chores. What an idiot he was for hiring her back in the first place. Then again, he hadn't expected her to take him up on the offer. It was yet another miscalculation where the feisty redhead was concerned. He was beginning to think she really was his equal in the game of mental manipulation.

Which left him only one advantage. The bedroom. Or anywhere else he chose to enforce her slavery. And she was still his slave, whether she wanted to admit it or not. That kind of thing didn't change with a job promotion. Especially not as deep as he'd gotten into her psyche.

Trouble was, she'd gotten into his, too, and now there was no separating out his feelings from his reason.

Oh, god, she was back, that cute little pout of hers still locked on her face and that fearsome little wiggle of defiance in her hips. She was so adorable when she was angry. So eminently...fuckable. Though she didn't know it, it was his influence, and more importantly his strong, safe presence that was allowing her to release some of those feelings.

Even if they were all coming out against him.

"What about the Wilshire projections?" he demanded as she handed him the coffee.

"Not ready yet. I'll have them for you tomorrow."

"Negative, Miss Hunter. You'll give them to me tonight." Wilder took a sip of the coffee, instantly spitting it across the room. "What the—"

"Problem, sir?" Meridian tried to suppress her smirk.

He tossed the cup into the wastebasket and reached for her.

"Let go of me," she squealed as he hooked his arm around her waist.

"I told you once before," he drew her across his lap. "When you act like a child, I will treat you like one."

She tried to put her hands behind her to protect herself.

He pinched her ass hard. "Don't fight me or it will go a lot worse for you."

"I'll scream," she cried. "I'll have you arrested."

"No," he said with a degree of authority that surprised even him. "You will take your punishment, like a good employee."

Meridian relaxed, though she took the opportunity to remind him how much she despised him.

He flipped up her skirt. She was damp and fragrant and he was hard as a rock. It was going to be a challenge keeping this platonic. "Do you know why I'm doing this?" He rested his hand, possessive and casual on the delicious curve of her behind.

The blue panties twitched. "Because you're a sadistic son of a bitch?"

He fought back a smile. "No, Meridian. It's because I don't want you to carry around the scars of the actions you perform against me. In being punished, I release you."

"How convenient for you," she scorned. "All I can say is, there'd better be one hell of a Christmas bonus in all this."

Wilder raised and lowered his hand. Hard and efficient but not cruel. God, it was as if he was made to discipline this woman. To keep her in line, to...

He swallowed, delivering another swat. He'd nearly said he was made to love her. But that was not a possibility. Not now. Not ever.

"How many?" he inquired, trying to keep his concentration. "How many should I give you?"

She did her best to effect a cool, sarcastic veneer. "As many as you can handle... I assume this is supposed to be hurting you worse than me?"

"I do not appreciate being mocked." He delivered another measured blow. Damn, her ass felt so good under his hand. He wanted it naked, wanted to see the squirming, the wriggling, unencumbered by her underwear.

Meridian winced. "And I don't appreciate being...beaten."

His cock swelled against her pelvis. This had to end quickly, or not at all. "Just tell me you've learned your lesson and we'll be done with it."

"Oh, I've learned plenty. Next time no salt in your coffee—soap instead."

"You really don't want a future with me, do you? With my company?"

"Sure I do," she challenged. "But I'll have it on my terms. Taking all you can dish out and more."

"You can't defeat me," he grasped the woman's posterior.

"Already have," she countered. "You just don't know it."

He lifted her off of him. "That will be all, Miss Hunter."

"What about that?" Her green eyes tipped in the direction of his surging erection. "Don't you want me to take care of it for you? Or isn't that part of the little supervisory arrangement you've just worked out? Face it, Wilder, you've lost perspective."

Marshall really wanted to have something to throw back at her, except the woman wasn't doing anything wrong. Other than to dig at his emotions in vastly uncomfortable ways. "That will be all," he repeated. "You are dismissed, Miss Hunter."

He watched her go to the door, lock it and come back. A moment later she was in front of him, her green eyes lit like emeralds. "All right, Wilder, it's time to get to the bottom of this. I want to know, what is your problem with me?"

They were nearly the same words he'd once used on her.

"None. As long as you do your job. Properly and efficiently."

"But you don't really want that," she countered. "You want me to make mistakes. You want me dependent. Off-balance. You want…this."

"This" was the body underneath the gray tweed skirt, which she unbuttoned and allowed to fall to the floor.

Wilder clenched a clammy fist at the sight of the young woman's panties. "Miss Hunter, put your clothes on. Get out."

She slithered the panties down her hips. "No," she rasped. "Sir."

Meridian wore high black heels, open-toed, her nails painted a sexy pink. One by one she lifted her feet to take off the lilac underwear. "Here's my report," she tossed them onto his desk under his nose. "Submitted for your approval."

He sucked in a breath. It was all he could do not to leap from the seat, grab the woman and throw her down on the couch for the fucking of her life. "You're playing with fire, young lady."

"I've already been burned," the redhead tossed her head. "Remember?"

"I hired you back because you're the right woman—the right person—for the job. You are qualified. Always have been. You understand that?"

"Oh, I know that." She was unbuttoning her blouse, maddeningly, slowly. "And I'm here offering myself because you're the man for *this* job."

The blouse fluttered to the floor. Her bra was lilac like the panties. Full breasts strained at the laughably thin material. To see her like this was to want not only to take and have her once more, but to own and control definitively. He also wanted to push her to her natural limits.

"I make love only on my own terms," he warned. "You know that."

She licked her lips. "I understand."

His heart pounded in his chest. He was determined, hell-bent on showing her more, though why he had no clue. Opening his desk drawer he found a pair of large, silver paper clips. In a feat of inspiration, he bent each of them out, forming a tiny A-frame that could be tightened or loosened at will.

"Put these on," he commanded, tossing them to the floor at her feet.

Meridian crouched down, still in her heels, retrieving the jury-rigged nipple clamps. She looked at them and took a deep breath. "How tight?" she whispered.

"As tight as I want."

Merry's face went soft and slack, her submissive core touched by his dominant words. Standing before him, her eyes forward, she reached behind her for the bra strap. Wilder rubbed his crotch lightly. His cock was straining to burst free. It would be torture for him, as well, this extended, semi-sadistic foreplay.

Meridian was smart enough to understand what she must do. Her nipples were more than ready, full and swollen. She looked so sweet, so serious and lovely as she applied the first one, taking care to push it far enough to the back of her nipple so as to keep it in place. Bending the metal over, she was able to tighten it on top of her sensitive nub.

"Tighter," he said at once. "Make it tighter."

Meridian released a small moan as she did so, as much from pleasure as pain. A moment later, she had completed the second nipple. Twice more, he had her tighten the metal, gradually, getting her used to the pressure.

"What do you want?" he asked, employing a phrase straight out of their so-called experiment.

"Your cock," she said, without hesitation, "in my pussy."

"Masturbate," he said instead, sliding a silver cigar tube forward on the surface of the desk. It was a rare *Cubano*, a gift from a client. "Use this to show me what it is you want me to do to you."

"Yes," she said, her voice a tight rasp.

Flushed and wanton, she was all woman. Her eyes had an eerie light as she retrieved the object and put herself in place to absorb it. Hooking one heel over the arm of the chair, she spread her pussy lips. They were wet, glistening. The liquid was already dripping down her thighs.

It was such a wicked thing to do. But he was ordering her to do it, and that made it sexy and irresistible.

Throwing back her head she released a controlled, heavy sigh as she put the cool, smooth aluminum against her clitoris. She was panting heavily, but trying desperately to keep from screaming.

"Make it good," he encouraged. "Earn your right to my cock."

The naughty, humiliating talk seemed to turn her on as much as what she was doing for him.

"Oh, god," she looked at him in lustful wonder. "What you…do to me."

"Tighten the clamps," he said. "I want you feeling that, too."

"Oh, M-M—"

Wilder stiffened in his chair. Had she been about to call him Marshall or Master?

"Lie down on the floor," he said huskily. "On your back on the rug. Legs spread. Wide. Keep touching yourself. Show me, show me how obedient you can be."

She did as she was told, the high-heeled beauty arranging herself as would any common whore. "Nnnnn," she grunted, using both hands to maneuver the tube.

"No coming," he reminded, "without permission."

"Oh, please," she whined, her eyes glazed over and hungry as he'd ever seen a woman before. "May I?"

"No. You have more to go. More to suffer." The words were difficult, but his tone was gentle, inviting and seductive. This was what they both needed, what they had both been missing in their lives.

"But…I have to have it," she whimpered.

"Pinch your nipple. Hard."

She did so, the pain utterly blended with pleasure.

"Yes," he said. "That's what I want to see. That's what pleases me. Don't hold back. Hips in the air. Harder."

She lifted her ass, heels dug in, wantonly thrusting toward the ceiling. He wanted in that picture so bad, the tight little needy body, hungry, undulating, writhing, the sweat-soaked wild hair, the ruby lips begging to be kissed into utter and complete submission.

But he would make her wait. It was…another lesson. Though it was unclear what was still to be learned, and by whom. Nor did he see an end to these desires of theirs anymore—his to control, hers to let him. He would have to cut this off. Once and for all. As soon as this little scene ended, that is.

"Roll over," he said, lost in the moment, lost in the intoxication of his power. "On your belly."

She moaned piteously. The position crushed her breasts, clamped and over sensitized as they were, beneath her. It also left her pussy under intense pressure from the impaling tube.

"Bounce," said her boss. "Bounce your ass."

The very word, so coarse and unsexy added to the humiliation. There was nothing sensual here, nothing graceful. He wanted her moving graphically, performing in a way that would as quickly as possible reduce her to something…inferior.

Meridian screamed into the rug. She was convulsing, but not yet orgasming. Leaving his seat, he went to her, ready to escalate her misery.

Ordering her to lift herself, he took the cigar tube. It would, he decided, make a fine anal plug.

"Bounce harder."

She made a deep rhythmic noise as he slipped the moist cylinder inside her anus, impaling her. Any man hearing such a sound, a Master in particular, couldn't help but be drawn in.

"You will never again after this make any sexual advances toward me," he informed her, realizing at once the absurdity of what he was saying under the circumstances. "If you do, I will make it much, much worse for you."

"Fuck me," she was saying, her voice half moan, half dry-throated gasp. "Please…Master."

Wilder's blood moved instantly to boil. "I told you, that is all over. I'm not your Master."

Not thinking clearly, he unzipped his pants, intent on punishing her, in setting her straight with his cock. As if this would not only make things more complicated and desperate between them.

"Say it with me," he sank his dick into her in one clean thrust. "I am not a slave. I have no Master. I am a free woman."

"MMMMMaster…" Meridian was orgasming. There wasn't a power in the cosmos that could stop her, not even the Great Energy Source itself.

Wilder himself was lost in this primal power. In a bold, overblown show of ego, he raced ahead, blasting from the end of his cock his own pent-up passions. He screamed with her, not giving a damn who heard.

There had to be a few perks to owning your own company, right?

They continued to ride the tide together, a long wave surging ever higher, cresting blue and white foam beneath a raw current of desire heading into a boundless shore. It was a thing of utter unity, yin and yang, possessor and receptacle. Conqueror and willing vessel. She'd never been more his slave, not even at the cabin, when she'd so clearly been at his tethered naked mercy.

Submission, as always, is a thing of the mind and it was clear from her responses she had reached this new place of peace, with herself and with life. But that did not necessarily mean anything had changed in him. In fact, it was quite the opposite.

Giving her no time to recuperate, he climbed off her, removed the "anal plug" and acted as if nothing had happened. "You'll be on the road next week," he told her. "There's a company in Denver I want you to look at. I'm thinking of buying it."

Tears clouded her eyes. Bubble burst. Mission accomplished.

"All right," she said weakly.

It was a new attitude from her. Resignation, maybe? Or had she finally cut the Gordian knot between them with the bloody blade he'd offered? It was good, a very good thing…so why did he feel a little…sad?

"I'll do it…Mr. Wilder." She was sitting up, looking for her clothes, trying to end the embarrassment as quickly as possible.

"Fine. I'll leave you to…" His voice trailed off to nothingness. He couldn't get out of the office fast enough. It was supposed to be his office, though he didn't feel particularly deserving of it at the moment. Or of anything else, for that matter.

This is all for her own good, he kept telling himself.

So why did he feel like such a complete heel?

Chapter Eight

"Okay, boss, this isn't working."

Meridian looked up at Kennedy, who had recently added some rather colorful blue streaks to her hair, a perfect match to her blue sundress and toenails.

"What isn't working?"

"This," she held out her well-toned, disgustingly youthful arms. "This whole 'I'm fine and over him and pouring myself into my work' routine."

Meridian scanned the top of her desk, buried in papers. "All this has to get done. And the buck stops with me," she declared.

Kennedy rolled her eyes then made a dramatic show of bowing, arms extended. "All hail," she pronounced. "Cleopatra, Queen of—"

Merrie held up her hand. "Don't say it."

She knew what was coming and there was no way she was going to let herself in for a lecture about her emotional life. She was over Marshall Wilder and that was that. To be precise, there had never been anything between them in the first place. Except for sex. And where did that ever get you in life?

"You can tune me out if you like, but you're going to have to confront him, you know that. And I'm not the only one who thinks so. The whole building knows it."

Merrie went pale. "Knows what?"

"That you and the boss man are playing Tracy and Hepburn. Cat and mouse. The oldest game in the book. There's a pool, if you must know."

"A pool?" She swallowed.

"On how long it takes 'til one of you cracks. I have a week from Thursday. I could really use the money, mind you, but I don't want to unduly influence you in any way."

Merrie buried her head in her hands. She'd hoped the trip to Denver would cool off the gossip. Apparently it had only added fuel to the fire. "Wonderful. My life has become an office joke."

"Actually, everyone's on your side. We figure you'll marry the jerk, clean his clock and take over the whole shooting match."

"He's not a jerk," she snapped. "Well…not that kind anyway."

Kennedy was smirking. Merrie blushed, caught in a blatant show of defending the man.

"Look, it's no big deal, okay, Kennedy? He's the boss, he's an honest man and we all work for him. End of story."

Kennedy broke out into a silly children's rhyme, teasing. "Merrie and boss man, sitting in a tree, k-i-s-s-i-n-g."

"Go," Merrie pointed to the door grimly, feeling more like Marshall Wilder every minute.

She waited until the young woman had closed the door before crying. It had been three days of waterworks since getting back to the office, and she hadn't thought she could cry anymore. Hell, she wasn't exactly sure why she'd cried in the first place. What exactly had she lost? It was all a blur. So many feelings, so fast. He was so new in her life and he'd taken on so many roles. Boss. Mentor. BDSM teacher. And…lover. That was the strangest part of all. Somewhere in the midst of all the fireworks, and all the kinky sex there had been real lovemaking. And that was the last thing in the world she had ever expected.

The worst thing about the whole experience as she looked back on it now was that it had felt unresolved somehow. Like they hadn't had a chance to follow things to the natural conclusion. Sure, they probably would have ended up hating each other and broken up in a week. But they hadn't gotten into it far enough. So much had poured over them so fast and it was all a big mess.

She was pretty sure he really had been just trying to protect her. Doing everything he could, crazy as it was, to push her away from him, from the BDSM lifestyle. Why he thought that he in particular was so bad for her, though, she hadn't a clue. Breaking it all down, detail by detail, it had all been good for her. He had taught her all manner of things about herself, he'd reached out, at least as far as he was capable at this point, and he gave her pleasure. Lord, did he give pleasure.

It just seemed so silly that they had broken up over that. She'd rather that they hadn't started anything in the first place. And where had she fit into it all? Had she given him a fair chance, or did she put so many expectations on him at different points that he'd ended up folding his hand? She didn't doubt he could handle her, but maybe she hadn't sent the signals she thought she had. Maybe she, too, was telling him at some level to keep away. Maybe she was using the sex, the play to make it impossible to get to know her as a person.

Oh, hell, it really was just impossible to know anything for sure.

But how could she get another chance? How could she take control back for the two of them in this relationship, let it find its own way, instead of being some absurd office pool. She couldn't see marrying him, but she couldn't see *not* marrying him either. In other words, there was nothing inherent to rule it out.

He made her feel good. They clashed, but also clicked and that was the Dance, after all, of love. They worked well together, too. These last few days had shown that. Granted, she'd had to twist his arm here and there, but there were no more salted coffee incidences, at least. In fact, they were actually tooling up this business and other ones too. She was learning from him, absorbing, and he was somehow…more mellow.

And they sure had shown themselves compatible in bed the few times they'd been together so far. He was the only man who'd ever realized her fantasies. More than that, he'd blown them out of the water with the reality. It was a tension, a feeling that pervaded everything even now. When their fingers inadvertently brushed while passing off a document, when they passed in the hall, him so much larger and stronger, looking down on her, protective. Shyly, she would lower her eyes and feel the heat in her loins. This meant something. It had, too. There were urges here.

And what about ownmenow and Master Nightshade? Had those two characters had a chance to fulfill their dreams and see where their relationship went? Those personas were real parts of them, they had brought something out in each other and that was a reality that simply could not, should not, be buried.

But how…how to reach him again after all this? The man was stubborn, more stubborn than she, if that was possible. And he would never backtrack, never open an old wound or risk putting her in what he thought was any kind of emotional jeopardy. He had her safe now, contained, in her job, acting rationally, and he would do nothing to upset that.

Unless…

Merrie's face lit with a slanted smile. A wicked idea had just come into her mind. A devious, wicked idea. More diabolical even than the little stunt he had pulled on her to connect them in the first place. So diabolical, in fact, that she was pretty sure it might work.

Reaching for her purse, she took out her lipstick. Passion pink. She would have to look her best for her little performance. Almost giddy, she buzzed Wilder to see if he was busy and asking if she could come round.

He said yes, she could, grudgingly.

Heart thumping, she rose to her feet. It was time for the CEO to have a little lesson of his own.

*****

Wilder grumbled at the thought of Miss Hunter paying him a visit right now. He really was not in the mood for any histrionics. Retreating to his mini-putting green, he took a measured stroke. Obediently, the tiny white ball sailed across the Astroturf, dropping satisfyingly into the hole. According to his new psychologist, this was good therapy for stress.

What Dr. Liebensraum didn't know yet, however, was that he was dealing on a daily basis with the most gorgeous, frustrating, yet talented woman of his life. And she was taking her toll, gradually wearing him down. Not to mention causing him to act like a hormone-struck teenager.

As usual, Miss Hunter hit from out of left field with her opening remarks. "Mr. Wilder, I am here to resign," she announced, with a flip of sparkling copper hair.

Marshall lined up another ball, determined to keep his cool. "If this is about the Kazimoto merger, I already told you it was merely a consideration, not a done deal. If you feel that strongly against it—"

"I've met someone else."

Wilder gripped the putter. "Oh?"

Theoretically, this should be good news. How many times had he said he'd wanted rid of the responsibility of watching over her love life? Not to mention the burden of looking at her single self each day and not being able to have her for his own.

"I'm surprised you have had the time," he quipped, not bothering to look at her. "As hard as you've been working."

"I met him online," she offered cheerfully.

Wilder drew a cleansing breath. What was it Liebensraum had told him? Count to ten before reacting emotionally?

"Online. You don't say."

"Through the site," she nodded. "You know, the Xchange?"

"Oh? I wasn't aware you were still using it…after our experiment."

"Yes…well, I didn't intend to act on anything at first, but it just kind of happened. He's a Dominant…a very interesting man… I think you'd like him actually."

"Actually," he whirled to face her, the whole counting thing shot to hell. "I haven't any interest in your personal life. If you choose to live it with or without the Xchange, that is your concern."

"I'm in love, Marshall. I have found my love Master."

His lips thinned. "Meridian, I can't make this any clearer…"

"I am going to be with him. He owns a yacht and a villa in the Bahamas. He's the man for me and I'm going to live with him. As his property, forever."

The blood was pounding in his head. All his work, blown to smithereens. One smart-talking smooth operator and this vulnerable, naïve woman was completely off-track, about to be sold down the creek without a paddle. "Meridian, I am not sure you've really thought this through. I mean, how long have you known him?"

"What does that matter?" She challenged. "Love can be at first sight. I've read it in all the women's magazines and seen it on TV, too. He's my soul mate. Anyway, he's already put his collar on me. We had an online ceremony and everything."

Marshall tried to hold his temper. "For god's sake, Meridian, life is not some foolish magazine or a talk show. Did you absorb nothing I shared with you? Online is fantasy, pure drivel. Hell, even reality isn't real."

She folded her arms, cocksure. "Well, like you said, it makes no difference to you. I just wanted you to know. Thought maybe you'd be happy for me. My new slave name is firegirl, by the way."

Wilder pointed his finger at her, CEO style. "Meridian, I forbid this. You will not go with this man. You will not, in fact, leave this office until—"

"Until what?" She poked back, striking his chest. "'Til you've finished beating your breast like Tarzan? You had your chance with me, big boy, and you blew it. You didn't want me, remember? I wasn't good enough for you. So I found someone to appreciate me, and now you're jealous. Talk about pathetic."

"Who is this man, Meridian? What is his handle? I demand to know!"

"Why?" She taunted. "Why do you care? I'm nothing to you. Just an employee…right?"

"I happen to care about my employees, that's all."

She snorted. "Well that would be a first."

"How dare you?" he bellowed. "You've no right to say such a thing."

"I have every right in the world," she smiled coldly behind freshly painted lips. "Because you don't own me. Goodbye, Marshall, it's been…interesting."

Wilder watched her leave, the pert, insolent posterior walking out of his door and out of his life. He collapsed onto the sofa, feeling like a heavyweight boxer who had just been knocked in the solar plexus.

Had what he thought happened, really happened? Did Meridian Hunter just waltz in, kiss him off and throw him over for some armchair Dominant, or worse still some Internet predator psycho?

I've got to pull myself together, he grimaced. *This is no time to fall apart.* Making it as far as the intercom, his head swimming, he called for security. "Wilder here. Meridian Hunter is on the way down. Detain her."

There was a hesitation on the other end of the line. "Detain her, sir?"

The vein in his temple was pulsing. "Yes, damn it, detain her. Cuff her, drag her to a broom closet, whatever the hell it takes to keep her here 'til I get down there. And it's all your jobs on the line if she gets away."

"Yes, sir. Right away, sir."

Wilder clicked off. He had no idea what the hell he would say to her, just that he was going to get the last word. Even if that meant a four letter one.

* * * * *

Merrie's plan was working a little too well. The guards were redder-faced than their jackets, clearly embarrassed at having been ordered to hold her prisoner. Whatever nerve she'd touched off in their boss, it apparently rivaled the potency of a small nuclear warhead and she did not want to see them losing their jobs in the fallout.

"I'm sorry, Miss Hunter," said the dark-haired one as he and two others ushered her to the conference room on the first floor. "This will only take a moment, I'm sure."

"We appreciate your cooperation," added the other one, his eyes just begging her not to run and sue for false detention. "I'm sure Mr. Wilder will be right down."

"It's quite all right," she assured them. "I'm a big girl. I can amuse myself while I'm waiting."

Marshall came down a few minutes after the guards left.

"Well, there's a new wrinkle in your employee relations program," she greeted him. "Retention by kidnapping. What's next? Being stretched on the rack?"

Marshall's features were dark and sullen, though his eyes were wild like his name. "I'm not going to let you throw your life away, Meridian."

"I have needs, Marshall. You know I do. I can't help how I'm made. I'm a submissive woman. You taught me that."

He ran his hands through his hair in an act of utter exasperation. "Don't throw my own words in my face, dammit. You know what I was trying to do with you."

"Actually," she confronted him. "I don't. Why don't you tell me? First you lie to me to make me fall for you so you can humiliate me. Then when I run away, like any sane woman, you pursue me and seduce me. But as soon as I show the slightest interest in what you're doing to me, you drop me like a hot potato. Just exactly what would you call that? Other than just plain fucking with my head."

"I just wanted to..."

She could see it there on the tip of his tongue. Just let it out, damn you!

"To what?" She pushed at him. Literally. Anything to break into that fortress of his, and get at some real human emotions.

He pulled her hands off his chest by the wrists. "This isn't helping things, Meridian."

She had to laugh. "Helping what? I don't even know what's going on. Why am I even here? Why did you have your men stop me? Don't you want me out of your life? I know you do. You make it painfully obvious every day. I'm a burden. A little slave wannabe underfoot, like a charity project. Isn't that right, Marshall?"

"Yes, that's it. Exactly. And I have officially had enough." His face was stone. "It ends now. I hope you and your new Master are very happy together. I hope you enjoy licking his boots the rest of your life. Whoever he turns out to be."

Meridian felt her plan, her life exploding in her face. She hadn't been able to goad him into admitting a damned thing. Hell, maybe he really was the heartless robot he pretended to be.

The tears weren't something she'd bargained on. A cascade of them, welling up in her eyes, flooding her cheeks and pouring to her chin. Her shoulders were shaking and her lips quivering, but no words were coming out.

Oh, how she hated being a woman at times like this.

Wilder gathered her instinctively into his arms. It was just the kind of man he was. No matter what had gone on between them, he would never let her just be in pain like that.

It was one of the reasons she loved him. Had she told him that lately? She'd tried it twice before, but he'd dismissed it, as a slave thing, some inner subspace mumbo jumbo that couldn't be real. But this was different. She was in her right mind, on her own turf.

"Marshall, I need you to listen to me. Very closely." Never had she felt this strongly, this sure of herself. And yet, in what she was about to do, she would be admitting something, making herself vulnerable in a way she had never even dreamed possible. "We've been round and round this, you and I. I've laughed and cried. I've lost more sleep than I can ever get back. I'm so mixed up, I don't know if I am coming or going half the time. But I know one thing. I belong to you."

Marshall tried to push her away, but she held fast. "I do, Marshall Wilder. I am yours. And whether or not you ever take me, I will stay yours. The rest of my life. It's something you can't control, can't wish away, sell or merge, it just is. I love you, and that's a fact."

He frowned, his eyes intent. "What about your new Master?"

"I made him up. To get us…here."

His brow furrowed. "I should spank you for that."

She laughed, the tension dissipating. "I wish to hell you would."

He sighed, releasing her. "Meridian, there is so much you don't know about me. I'm not the man you think. You want some Master from your dreams, but I have feet of clay. I drive people away. I'm demanding, I'm stubborn, I'm—"

She put her finger to his lips. "Hush. You think you could possibly tell me anything I haven't already figured out on my own? Besides, who wants a perfect Master? Then I'd have to be a perfect slave."

He shook his head. "The kind of things you've read about, fantasized, they can't be lived out that way."

"I hope not," she smiled. "Wouldn't that make life boring? I want to be surprised, every step of the way, don't you?"

He blinked, eyes moist. "I'm just not sure…"

"Sure of what?" She pressed. "Of the price of the Dow next month? Whether we'll have children, what?"

"Yes—that and everything else. Meridian, I don't know what I can offer you. My god, I can promise the world to anyone else, but with you, everything just falls apart. I can't…keep it together."

She grasped his chin, making him look directly into her eyes. "You're not supposed to, silly. Just answer me one question. Do you love me? Tell me you don't and I will walk out of your life forever."

He sighed deeply. "No," he replied at last, his voice raspy and deep. "I can't say that I don't love you…in fact…"

Merrie couldn't wait for the words to come out. Leaping up on tiptoes, she planted a big wet kiss on his lips. "Master," she whispered.

"My angel," he whispered back. "My sweet, sweet angel… I do love you. I do."

* * * * *

Meridian stirred her drink, the pink swizzle stick clanking against the pale ice. She was wistful, somewhat sleepy, but also deeply…expectant.

"This is from the gentleman," the bartender slid a fresh scotch in front of her.

She followed the incline of the bartender's head to the man way down at the end of the polished surface, a lacquered cherry wood that dimly reflected the soft glow of the chandeliers. The hotel bar was empty at present save for the three of them and she'd noticed since this second customer's entrance how he'd been watching her. Sizing her up as it were, trying her out.

"Tell him I couldn't possibly—"

"Accept?" said the man, who had somehow managed to sidle up on her opposite side. "And why not? Afraid you'd be under obligation?"

"No," she replied boldly. "I just didn't want you wasting your money."

The dark-haired man smiled. "Oh? So you're that sure I won't be able to charm my way into your bed?"

She sipped from his scotch, savoring her victory. "Honey, I'm so sure, I'll let you take your best shot and if I'm not one hundred percent turned off I'll go with you right now and do whatever you want, all night. But if I am turned off, then you'll pay me a thousand dollars, which I know is pocket change to a man like you."

The ruggedly handsome man in the tuxedo laughed, dry as a martini. "Well that's hardly a fair wager, is it? How do I know you won't simply pretend to be turned off just to get the money?"

She licked her lips, a quick little dart between her teeth. "Do I look like the kind of woman who'd lie?"

His eyes flicked up and down with admirable discreteness over her highly aroused body, the lineaments of which were ill-disguised in the small, tight red dress. It was a fire engine red, a nice contrast to her well-combed and more subdued copper-colored hair.

"A woman like you doesn't have to lie," he crooned, his voice sending chills down her spine.

"Hmm," she sighed. "I can see I am liable to lose this bet after all."

"How about a new bet, then? Something a little more…sporting, shall we say?"

"What did you have in mind?" Meridian was already squirming, her thighs moist in anticipation. She wanted more from the man, a lot more.

He pulled a money clip from his inner jacket pocket "I will give you a thousand dollars if you tell me what you are thinking, at this very moment."

Now it was her turn to laugh. "And how do you know the thoughts in my head are worth anything close to that kind of money?"

He downed the shot in front of him and placed a thousand dollars on the table. "Oh, they are, all right, assuming you are as honest with me as your beauty compels."

She pursed her lips, feeling mischievous. "All right. I'll play your little game. I am, at this moment, thinking of you, and wondering...what your kisses taste like."

The man nodded. "A clever answer. But incomplete."

She reached for the thousand. "I'm afraid you'll have to take my word for it."

His hand intercepted hers, covering it. "Not so fast, my dear."

Meridian felt his knee pressing at hers. Reflexively, she looked down, just as he'd intended. He'd unbuttoned the tuxedo jacket to reveal a silver pistol, sleek and very modern.

She gasped. "You're..."

"A white slaver," he shrugged. "Guilty as charged. An old breed, I'm afraid. My great-grandfather was a pirate. Specialized in taking young maidens such as yourself at sea."

"I will scream if you touch me."

"I won't need to. As you see, I have a gun. Although I won't need to use it, seeing as you're more the deer in front of headlights variety. We'll be upstairs in my suite ten minutes before you even know what hit you," he smiled.

Indeed, she offered no resistance as he guided her by the elbow from the lounge and out to the elevator.

"Why are we going upstairs?" She asked logically. "If you intend to kidnap me?"

His smile was a bit sheepish. "I'm afraid I've a bit of a taste for the wares, so to speak. I'm going to have my way with you before the pickup crew arrives."

Meridian's heart began to thump like a rabbit's. It hadn't really dawned on her until now what was at stake. "Sir, you don't even know me, but I promise you—"

"Oh, don't worry," he cut her off. "I will know you. Very soon."

She had yet to mount any resistance as he took her from the elevator. Was this one of the things these men looked for? Weakness in a woman's eyes? Evidence that she was aroused by such treatment, and therefore unlikely to offer protest?

The man locked the door behind her and slid the chain. "Would you like a drink?"

Meridian looked around the room. A set of stocks had been set up and a steel rack with shackles dangling from the top. An assortment of whips, clamps and other devices for restraint sat on the desk. Even the bed had been fashioned for torture, with Velcro straps in each of the four corners and a large wooden paddle resting on one of the pillows.

"Sir, I beg you," said the increasingly panicked woman. "Don't do this."

"There's no point resisting," he poured a pair of scotches. "As you can see, this has all been quite well thought out."

"I can pay you money," she tried to keep the terror from her voice. "I'm not rich, but I have some savings. Twenty thousand. Twenty-five, counting the bonds."

"Drink," he soothed, putting the amber liquid to her lips.

She opened, taking the strong liquor into her mouth and down her throat. It burned her tummy, instantly opening her.

"Good." He smiled approvingly as she drank it all down. "Now take your clothes off."

"Sir, please...you don't want to hurt me do you?"

Her handsome abductor had a riding crop. She had not seen him pick it up. "Actually," he whistled it through the air. "I do. Now I am going to ask you again, politely, and after that, I won't be responsible for my actions. Is that clear?"

She took a step backward. "Sir, you wouldn't tear the clothes from me, would you?"

He arched a brow considering. "Actually," said Meridian's husband, "I would, but I'd prefer not to, as I am only going to have to pay for its replacement."

Wilder's bride arched an eyebrow of her own, more delicate, finer, but every bit as potent. "The hell you say," she challenged, having followed his lead in breaking out of character. "I will pay for it out of my own pocket, thank you very much. I may be many things to you, Marshall Stanton Wilder," she put her hands on her hips. "But a kept woman is not one of them."

"What you are is my helpless slave girl," Wilder growled playfully, swooping in. Gathering her in his arms he tossed her onto the king-sized bed. Though they'd never been in this particular room, in this particular bed, by the carefully arranged rules of their marriage, the turf was his.

Between the sheets, he ruled with an iron fist.

"You don't fight fair," she pouted.

Wilder had her pinned. His heart was beating fast, his pupils were dilated. She could feel his hard cock. Playing their little capture games never failed to arouse him to a crescendo of dominant passion. She didn't exactly hate them either. It was a beautiful symbiosis, a chance to engage each other's deepest primal needs. And it left other areas intact. Areas where they needed to work hand in glove. Like in the business. They were partners there and he had no problem with that because in the last six months since they'd been married, she'd made him more money than the last three years combined.

But here, in this way, she would always need him to be the boss. The Master.

"You'd better be wet for me," he warned, pushing up the hem of her dress.

She smiled inwardly, knowing that would never ever be a problem in her department.

"I'm not easy," she informed him, goading him just for fun. "You'll have to work for it."

"You are for me," he thrust his hand into her panties to probe her pulsing pussy. The lips parted for him with ease. Expertly, he found and assessed the swelling of her clitoris.

She moaned in response. "Oooo...what you do to me."

"You are not wet enough, slave girl," he informed her.

"Master, I try my best..."

He flipped her over onto her belly. Pulling up the dress, he proceeded to lay a series of precise sharp blows on her quivering buttocks. "I don't want excuses," he replied in his best CEO voice. "I want action."

"Yes, Master."

"Now..." He touched her clit again, getting her revved. "What do you intend to do about it?"

Merrie stretched her arms in front of her. "I intend...to give you pleasure, Master."

She writhed for him, undulating her back.

"My standards are high, slave girl. And the consequences for disobeying me, severe."

"Oh, Master," she sighed, drawn into the words, the mutual fantasy. "What would you do to me?"

Shivers passed down her spine as she awaited the list. There was no end to the games to be played, the variety of things to be enjoyed.

"Cage you, for one thing. That would teach you your place. And give you to my security men. That would help you appreciate how lucky you are to serve only one man's pleasure."

"Oh, Master, I will try to be good for you."

"You're mine," he toyed with her sex. "Do you understand that?"

"Yes, Master."

"We rule an empire together, but behind closed doors you submit. To me and only to me."

"I...submit, Master," she groaned, her sex clenching around his finger, thirsting for his hard cock, needing the pressure, the penetration.

"Lie still," he chastised his wife. "You may not move without permission."

Meridian whimpered. Controlling her desire around this man was next to impossible, she had found, and yet more and more she was driven to obey him, to follow the urge to surrender, to find in herself the sweet, obedient slave. And he was the perfect man to bring it out, because he would never take advantage or in any way attempt to crush her spirit.

"Master...I can't...stay still."

He pulled aside the fabric of her panties and mounted her, his throbbing shaft descending into her silken depths, into that well-prepared channel he knew so well. Their clothes were still on—the urgency had been too great to delay even a moment longer. "You will lie still, or you will be subjected to a prolonged torture that will leave you begging for my slightest touch."

Truthfully, she was ready to do that now.

"Yes, Master."

His cock slid in and out of her thirsty hole. "I will be using you all night long," he informed her. "You will perform for me and satisfy me with exquisite pleasure."

"Yes," she cried. "I long to please you...I need to please you so much, Master."

"Wrap your legs," he commanded.

She locked her heels behind his taut ass, fusing their bodies, skin on skin, the temperature rising by the second. "Now," he indicated. "Hold onto me."

She did so, allowing him to take her on the ride of her life, strong measured strokes, hard as pistons, pounding her ass into the mattress. Wilder's eyes were dark, beyond intense. His cock was thicker than she ever remembered.

"Mine," he said through gritted teeth. "My woman."

"Oh, yes...yours." She could barely breathe, barely take in air, and yet at the same time she was soaring, high in the clouds.

He tore at the bodice of her dress to get at her breasts. She arched her back to give of herself. His teeth sank into her left breast, sucking tight, focusing almost immediately on the throbbing nipple. She held the back of his head, the spasms welling from deep within.

"Going to...come," she cried. He was beyond holding her back. She was his vessel, his conquered slave and his queen all at once. The look on his face, so sweet, so utterly masculine and satisfied pushed her over the brink. If she lived to be a hundred she would never see a sight so sweet. His cock pulsed out volley after volley into her waiting womanhood. She took it all, craving more.

"Ohhhhhhhh," she cried out, the orgasm overtaking her, lofting her high into an unknown sky and releasing her to sail down over rainbow clouds to a forgotten primeval earth. "Sooo...good."

For a few minutes afterward as he gathered himself, she enjoyed the simple pleasure of lying beneath him, knowing she had satisfied, truly satisfied the man she loved. How many females could say that in this world, knowing, believing they would always provide everything their man needed right at home?

Eventually, Wilder rolled onto his back.

"What's your pleasure, Master?" she whispered in his ear.

"Slave's choice," he mumbled sleepily.

She eyed his half-erect cock. In that case...

Pulling off her clothes, she knelt between his legs, licking him up and down, blowing softly, kissing and nibbling. His eyes were half-closed and his mouth was moving in a sweet way. He was so darling. In short order she had him at attention again. The very sight of that proud, powerful cock sent ripples of pleasure through her body.

What a specimen of masculinity. That narrow waist, the broad shoulders and thick biceps. A torso and muscled thighs that could have belonged to a man in his twenties. And yet he had so much experience beyond that age. Experience enough to rock her world and to own her heart.

Slave's choice, she thought, climbing over him to slide his penis into her waiting sex. She drew a sharp breath and pushed her palms onto his chest. Oh, yes. Oh, mother fucking yes.

He lay quite still as she commenced to riding him. Lifting herself, nearly to the tip, only to impale herself all over again. It was like having a series of shadow orgasms, pre-climaxes, all building to the real one. Faster and faster she went, so free and exhilarating. It was an amazing feeling, being in control and yet knowing the man was allowing this, that in reality he could and would take the power back whenever he liked.

Somehow that made it all the hotter, and more intense.

"Oh, baby," she moaned, her breasts jiggling in the air as she writhed. "Come with me."

His eyes popped open. He grasped her hips, a grin on his face. "Has my little slave girl been up to no good?"

"Yes," she looked at him with moist eyes. "Master."

He rode with her now. "We'll attend to that," he promised, "later."

They climaxed in tandem. Her moaning in joy, him grunting out his fresh conquest, their two bodies perfectly fit and complementary…again. It was thunder and rockets and soaring eagles, the crackling campfire in the forest, and a million things more besides. Their lives so intertwined, so much joy and hope between them.

"I love you," she murmured sometime later, nuzzled under the covers. "Master Nightshade."

"And I love you," he rasped. "ownmenow."

About the author:

Reese Gabriel is a born romantic with a taste for the edgier side of love. Having traveled the world and sampled many of the finer things, Reese now enjoys the greater simplicities; barefoot walks by the ocean, kisses under moonlight and whispers of passion in the darkness with that one special person.

Preferring to remain behind the scenes, cherished by a precious few, Reese hopes to awaken in the lives of many the possibilities of true love through stories of far off places and enchanted lives.

For the sake of love and hope and imagination, these stories are told. May they be enjoyed as much in the reading of them as in the writing.

Reese welcomes mail from readers. You can write to her c/o Ellora's Cave Publishing at 1337 Commerce Drive, Suite 13, Stow OH 44224.

Why an electronic book?

We live in the Information Age—an exciting time in the history of human civilization in which technology rules supreme and continues to progress in leaps and bounds every minute of every hour of every day. For a multitude of reasons, more and more avid literary fans are opting to purchase e-books instead of paperbacks. The question to those not yet initiated to the world of electronic reading is simply: *why?*

1. *Price.* An electronic title at Ellora's Cave Publishing runs anywhere from 40-75% less than the cover price of the exact same title in paperback format. Why? Cold mathematics. It is less expensive to publish an e-book than it is to publish a paperback, so the savings are passed along to the consumer.
2. *Space.* Running out of room to house your paperback books? That is one worry you will never have with electronic novels. For a low one-time cost, you can purchase a handheld computer designed specifically for e-reading purposes. Many e-readers are larger than the average handheld, giving you plenty of screen room. Better yet, hundreds of titles can be stored within your new library—a single microchip. (Please note that Ellora's Cave does not endorse any specific brands. You can check our website at www.ellorascave.com for customer recommendations we make available to new consumers.)

3. *Mobility*. Because your new library now consists of only a microchip, your entire cache of books can be taken with you wherever you go.
4. *Personal preferences are accounted for*. Are the words you are currently reading too small? Too large? Too...**ANNOYING**? Paperback books cannot be modified according to personal preferences, but e-books can.
5. *Innovation*. The way you read a book is not the only advancement the Information Age has gifted the literary community with. There is also the factor of what you can read. Ellora's Cave Publishing will be introducing a new line of interactive titles that are available in e-book format only.
6. *Instant gratification*. Is it the middle of the night and all the bookstores are closed? Are you tired of waiting days—sometimes weeks—for online and offline bookstores to ship the novels you bought? Ellora's Cave Publishing sells instantaneous downloads 24 hours a day, 7 days a week, 365 days a year. Our e-book delivery system is 100% automated, meaning your order is filled as soon as you pay for it.

Those are a few of the top reasons why electronic novels are displacing paperbacks for many an avid reader. As always, Ellora's Cave Publishing welcomes your questions and comments. We invite you to email us at service@ellorascave.com or write to us directly at: 1337 Commerce Drive, Suite 13, Stow OH 44224.

ELLORA'S CAVE
ROMANTICA PUBLISHING

Printed in the United States
29810LVS00005B/199-438